T0032084

Rakes of the Old Court

NORTHWESTERN WORLD CLASSICS

Northwestern World Classics brings readers
the world's greatest literature. The series features
essential new editions of well-known works,
lesser-known books that merit reconsideration,
and lost classics of fiction, drama, and poetry.
Insightful commentary and compelling new translations
help readers discover the joy of outstanding writing
from all regions of the world.

Mateiu Caragiale

Rakes of
the Old Court

A Novel

Translated from the Romanian by Sean Cotter

Northwestern University Press ✦ *Evanston, Illinois*

Northwestern University Press
www.nupress.northwestern.edu

Copyright © 2021 by Northwestern University Press. Originally published
in Romanian in 1929 under the title *Craii de Curtea-Veche*. Translator's
preface copyright © Sean Cotter. Published 2021. All rights reserved.

The translator gratefully acknowledges a grant from the PEN/Heim Translation Fund supporting this work.

Printed in the United States of America

10 9 8 7 6 5 4 3 2 1

Library of Congress Cataloging-in-Publication Data

Names: Caragiale, Mateiu I., 1885–1936, author. | Cotter, Sean, translator.
Title: Rakes of the old court : a novel / Mateiu Caragiale ; translated from
    the Romanian by Sean Cotter.
Other titles: Craii de Curtea–Veche. English | Northwestern world
    classics.
Description: Evanston, Illinois : Northwestern University Press,
    2021. | Series: Northwestern world classics | "Originally published in
    Romanian in 1929 under the title Craii de Curtea–Veche."
Identifiers: LCCN 2021008283 | ISBN 9780810142251 (paperback) | ISBN
    9780810143487 (cloth) | ISBN 9780810142268 (ebook)
Subjects: LCSH: Aristocracy (Social class)—Romania—
    Fiction. | Libertinism—Romania—Fiction. | Romania—Social
    conditions—20th century—Fiction.
Classification: LCC PC839.C34 C713 2021 | DDC 859.332—dc23
LC record available at https://lccn.loc.gov/2021008283

Que voulez-vous, nous sommes ici aux portes de l'Orient,
où tout est pris à la légère . . .
—Raymond Poincaré

CONTENTS

Dressed in a green frock, buttoned shoes, cape, and bowler hat, with his mustache waxed, face lightly powdered, and head held aloof, Mateiu stood out from the crowd on the streets of Bucharest, a Symbolist decadent lost in the Romanian capital. He kept his journal (written "only for myself") in French. He had a passion for heraldry, titles, and noble families, a drive many critics attribute to his extra-marital birth; his works often feature escutcheons and blazons, decorations that blend with his already highly ornamented writing. He was a self-conscious heir to Edgar Allan Poe, whose atmosphere he expands into a version of Romanian identity. *Craii de Curtea-Veche* (*Rakes of the Old Court*) is one of his four works (in addition to a novella, a collection of poetry, and a possibly unfinished detective story), the sum of which occupies 160 pages in the 1994 Romanian, scholarly edition. The small corpus was overshadowed in his lifetime by his father's vast dramatic work; the comic plays of Ion Luca Caragiale were heralded in their time, and he is the one honored with statues in front of the national theater in Bucharest. The father is, still today, "Caragiale," while the son is called "Mateiu" (the last letter mute).

Yet he has become much more than a parenthesis. While he enjoyed a handful of fanatic supporters during his lifetime, Mateiu suffered from his lack of readers, always too few in comparison with the broad appeal of his father's plays, and he died at age fifty in 1936. Over the rest of the century, his work gained importance. During the strictest Communist-era control of literary life, *Craii* was read, memorized in full, and even reenacted word-by-word by small cliques of "Mateists." His lush descriptions of ambiguity and secrecy provided contrast with and relief from the oppressive, bright optimism of 1950s socialist realism. While it received some scholarly attention under communism, the book and author would have to wait until after the events of 1989 to gain canonical status. Both Mateiu's and his father's works then enjoyed tremendous popularity, with *Craii* entering school textbooks, and his father's works spawning a political party. In 1995 the stately, decadent atmosphere of *Craii* was translated into a film. In 2001, a poll of more than one hundred literary critics chose *Craii* as the best Romanian novel ever written. *Craii* depicts a world of corrupt nobility, a Bucharest built on the ruins of an ancient castle, the "old court" of the title, one which housed only failed leaders. Despite its pessimistic surface, the work seduces its reader with its nostalgia for ruins, its passion for shimmering imaginary visions, its moments of scandalous coarseness, and its sympathy for vulnerable, lost personages. The book offers atmosphere, but few events: in 1910, four characters (three with names and one narrator) move through Bucharest mansions, bars, brothels, and convents, drinking and gambling among tragic characters and intriguing antiques. Their families are storied and mysterious; their conversations include elaborate descriptions of voyages around the world and into the past; and in the end, their bond is destroyed by the lives they lead. Rather than its action or characters, the book is prized above all for its ornate style, filled with archaic Romanian and base street language, saturated with Turkish, Roma, German, and Greek vocabulary. The novel's style provides ample demonstration of the complicated history of Romania, a nation at the crossroads of dead empires—the Ottoman, Russian, and Austro-Hungarian. All this complexity flows through the serpentine, opulent sentences, glittering in conflicting linguistic inheritances. The text resembles the turtle, in Huysmans's *À rebours*, that Esseintes covers in jewels—the novel constitutes a melancholy, reptilian world, lavishly ornamented in language.

The best introduction to the book's ornate aesthetic is a famous passage from the beginning, a passage that Mateiu repeats almost word for word at the end. Pașadia, Pirgu, Pantazi, and the narrator are dining in a restaurant, when a band begins to play:

> I would have started conversation, if the musicians had not
> begun precisely that waltz for which Pantazi had a weakness, a
> slow, dragging waltz, voluptuous and sad, almost funereal. In its
> mollitious oscillation, it traced a nostalgic and endlessly somber
> passion, one so rending that the very pleasure of listening to it
> became a kind of suffering. When the taut violin strings began to

mimic a careworn confession, the entire hall, in profound enchantment, fell mute. Ever darker, lower, and slower, describing dolor and deception, wandering and pain, rue and regret, the song, suffocated in nostalgia, drifted away, withered into a whisper, to a lost, tardy, and pointless cry.

The passage turns away from the social and toward the aesthetic, as the narration turns away from conversation, toward this long description of the oscillations and tautness that create the effect of nostalgia, the artistry which resolves only in it its own decay and pointlessness. In a similar way, the novel turns away from its characters and toward its style, even as this style risks collapsing under its own weight. Mateiu's rhetorical excess leads to a Romanian so exoticized that, even for many native speakers, it becomes illegible.

By the date of the book's publication in 1929, the modern state of Romania is only eleven years old and only sixty-three years out of Ottoman domination. We may read Mateiu's self-defeating rhetorical virtuosity as his indictment of the young nation. As Katherine Verdery observes, becoming a Romanian intellectual has long meant participating in debates on national character. Mateiu's position in this debate is pessimistic, and he creates a portrait of Romania by exploiting etymologies in the Romanian language. The novel's opening parodies the first lines of the national anthem, "Deșteaptă-te, române, din somnul cel de moarte" ("Awaken, Romanian, from the sleep of death"). Recovering consciousness after the previous night of drinking, the narrator uses particular terms to describe himself: "when my sleep is disturbed, I am . . ." and here follow three synonyms for "mean": *mahmur, ursuz, ciufut,* all three of evident Turkish origin. And they are all ugly, not only semantically, by virtue of the fact that they describe an unpleasant feeling, but also etymologically. We can hear that "*ciufut*" includes "Jew"; the word is antisemitic and in Romanian has a connotation of stinginess. So it is not just etymology that is interesting to Mateiu, but specifically those words which demonstrate unpleasant aspects of the narrator's character and (what he describes as) the character of Romania.

Mateiu's argument in this performance is transparently orientalist: all these Turkish words demonstrate that Romania is too close to the East to do more than wallow in bars and brothels. While other Central European novelists, such as Gregor von Rezzori or Miklós Bánffy, might lament the departure of the old empire, Mateiu feels Romania has no golden age to stir his nostalgia. When the narrator turns toward the past, he sees only the East: "Bucharest had remained faithful to its old norms of decrepitude, with every step we recalled that we were at the gates of the Orient." This type of diagnosis is not unique among Romanian intellectuals of the time, and since many writers were much more active participants in cultural politics, Mateiu's commentary on the nation did not significantly impact that debate. Nor was it designed to inspire social action. His novel turns away from the social; it is its own end, the decaying refuge from a world in decay. The most significant thing his works do inspire is reperformance, whether in the ritualistic recitals of the Mateists; the 1995 film; the 2008 audiobook, read by the prestigious philosopher Andrei Pleşu; or the miraculous, massive, and apocryphal collection *The Last Writings of Mateiu Caragiale, Accompanied by His Unpublished Correspondence, with an Index of Beings, Things, and Events, Presented by Ion Iovan*, published in Bucharest in 2009 to great acclaim; or Răzvan Luscov's picto-poem illustrated version from 2015, an image from which graces the cover of this translation.

My translation follows a tradition of reperformances. I have, however, one handicap that the others may avoid: my re-creation cannot use Mateiu's Romanian. *Craii* is so thoroughly written in Romanian, so much "about" the Romanian language itself, that translating it risks taking all the salt from the food. To choose just one aspect: English has no equivalent storehouse of Turkish words for me to use. As Aron Aji, an accomplished translator from Turkish, once told me, "You can only write 'yoghurt' so many times." But the goal of a translation is not to reproduce the original; rather, it is to create a text that makes an interesting comparison with the original. I can create grounds for this comparison by adopting Mateiu's characters, plot, and aspects of his method: his antiquarianism, his striving for rhetorical effect, and his juxtaposition of etymologies. I was guided by many years of reading paleo-modernists such as

T. S. Eliot and James Joyce, especially Eliot's translation of St.-John Perse, and I looked for clues in existing translations of Huysmans and Baudelaire. I consulted Claude Levenson's French translation of Mateiu, and I studied the cadences of speech in the film version, in particular those of Mircea Abulescu as Paşadia and Răzvan Vasilescu as Pirgu.

In working on etymologies, I focused on Latinate words, particularly uncommon words that create tension in English. While I don't imagine they will suggest images of Roman decadence or the reach of Rome's empire to England, I hope that the discomfort they create comes from the sense they are too ornate, un-Germanic, excessive. My principal procedure for finding these words was to troll through *The Oxford English Dictionary*. I began by simply searching for and scrolling through words in the main dictionary, but my work became much easier once I had access to the historical thesaurus. At one point in the novel, a character is sent out of the country for schooling, in part because the schools are better abroad, but more because the family wants to steal his inheritance. The Romanian says that for his schooling he is "*surghinuit*," a word of Turkish origin, meaning "exiled." I considered using "exiled," because it was Latin already. But it is also a common word. I can create more tension if I write he was "exsputed to another country for his education." That's unusual, and it also sounds old. The effect does not depend on my remaining consistent with this as an equivalent for "*surghinuit*," and when later the same root appears as a substantive, "*surghinuire*," I translate it as something else. I am not looking for word-for-word equivalences, but the creation of a comparable style.

Spurred by moments like "exsputed," I sought out other places in the translation to use Latinate words. Since Romanian is a Romance language, it provides many opportunities, including moments where the original is not at all unusual. "*Moale*" is simply "soft," but I have sometimes translated the word as "mollicious." At another point, a group of people are called "*îmbuibate*," which could be rendered "stuffed," but I chose "superalimented." Ravenous for English solutions, my own translation became superalimented on Latinate words. In the example quoted above, I matched "*duioşii şi dezamăgiri*" not with "pain and disappointment" but with "dolor and deception," which is both more Latinate and older. As we can see in that paragraph, this last phrase comes in a parallel construction with "rue and regret." I mean the Old English "rue" to exist in tension with the three Latinate words around it, as part of the description of the waltz, a description of music that is held together by its own music.

"Dadaists, Surrealists, Hermetics"—in a classic history of Romanian literature, this is the chapter that includes Mateiu. More than one sympathetic Romanian speaker, in appreciation of the original text's complexity, has asked whether I am translating Mateiu into Romanian. I have been grateful for guidance from Stavros Deligiorgis, Cosmin Ciotloş, and the Ro > En Translators group. Bogdan Suceavă's explanations of Pirgu's obscenities merit the Order of the Stone Cross. The *Massachusetts Review* gave a home to chapter 1, and a grant from the PEN/Heim fund gave the project a crucial boost. The idea to include notes belongs to Anne Gendler, the book's brave and generous copy editor, who also suggested many of the entry terms. Joan and Barry Cotter, my loving parents, have been curious and attentive readers of this project from its first drafts, over a decade ago, to its final version. In addition to the many positive reactions to my translation, I have kept in mind two principled negative readings: one suggested I use even more unusual and antiquated words, because the English sounded too "neutral," while the other urged me to rein in the rhetorical effects, because "it sounds like wretched Vincent Price." I value even contradictory strong reactions, and I recognize that my approach is far from the only one possible for translating Mateiu. In comparison with the Romanian version, *Rakes of the Old Court* (in English) is probably less coarse, as a result of its antiquarianism. Some words lose their menace as they get older; are we as worried by "rakes" as by "seducers"? Perhaps Pirgu's dialogue and destiny will still disturb us in the English version. Perhaps this re-creation of Mateiu's music, "so rending that the very pleasure of listening to it became a kind of suffering," will lead to further re-creations, further steps in the complicated history of this novel.

Rakes of the Old Court

Rakes' Congress

. . . au tapis-franc nous étions réunis.

—L. Protat

Even though I had sworn an oath the previous evening, to myself, to return early, I arrived home even later than usual: the next day, toward noon.

Evening found me horizontal, having lost all sense of time. I would have stayed fast asleep, were it not for a letter that arrived with a ruckus, begging a signature. When my sleep is disturbed, I am groggy, inconversable, costive. I refused to sign. I moaned that I should be left alone.

I dozed again, for a moment. The blasted epistle again materialized, now accompanied by raw lamplight. The villainous postman had deemed it meet to sign for me with his own hand. I showed no gratitude.

I loathe letters. As long as I have lived, I cannot say I have received more than one—from my good friend Uhry—that brought me happy news. I have a fear of letters. In those days, I would burn them without opening.

This fate awaited the newly arrived. Recognizing the hand, I could guess the message. I knew it by heart—that saltless home-cooked fish-bake of counsel and hounding served up the first of each month, the counsel to set myself on some career like a man, the nagging to reform myself. And in closing, the never-absent wish that God will keep His watch over me.

Amen! In the mood I found myself, it would have been beyond my powers to set on any path at all. I could not even move in the bed. My joints dismantled, my lower back in agony, I felt like stewed pig. Into my fogged mind came the fear I was suffering some palsy.

But I was not, and in the end I overcame my state. For a month, without a word or murmur, with hope and motive, I had been going out—for some drinks, some rakery, some play. In the years previous, I had been sorely tried by my circumstances, my tiny raft battered by great waves. I defended myself ineptly, and disgusted by everything beyond measure, I strove to find, within a life of debauchery, oblivion.

I took things a little quickly, however, and soon saw myself forced to lay down arms. I was completely drained. That evening, I felt finished, such that I could not imagine moving were the house to take flame. But I found myself suddenly in the middle of the room, on my feet, looking anxiously at the clock. I had remembered I was invited to eat with Pantazi.

What luck I had awoken, what great luck! I was grateful now for my parents' letter: without it, I would have missed a date with my dearest friend.

I dressed and went out. A night toward winter, an air of tears. Even though there had been no rain, everything was wet. The gutters wept, the branches stripped of leaves dripped fat drops, running down trunks and window grills like a cold sweat. This was the season that drove one above all to the bottle; the few passersby who drizzled through the fog were almost all drunk. One gangly boy, descending the steps of a bar, fell to the ground in a heap and did not move again.

I turned my head in disgust. Since the establishment selected for this evening sat on Str. Covaci, I took a hansom. It proved to be the right choice, since, on my arrival, the guests were already on their second round of ţuica and he who guested us, his third. I was surprised everyone had materialized so early; Pantazi explained he had come straight from home, while Paşadia and Pirgu from their club, the weather being too foul to dawdle over aperitifs.

Pantazi pronounced another round of ţuica. But the good cheer we wished each other, glasses clinking, was nowhere apparent. I feared I would fall asleep again. In the hall where a grotesque banquet of merchants and traders began to warm up—it was Saturday night—our table felt more like a wake.

The borscht, garnished with cream and a hot pepper, was sipped in silence. None of those sharing table raised their eyes from their bowls. Pirgu, especially, seemed to suffer a dark humor. I would have started conversation, if the musicians had not begun precisely that waltz for which Pantazi had a weakness, a slow, dragging waltz, voluptuous and sad, almost funereal. In its mollitious oscillation, it traced a nostalgic and endlessly somber passion, one so rending that the very pleasure of listening to it became a kind of suffering. When the taut violin strings began to mimic a careworn confession, the entire hall, in profound enchantment, fell mute. Ever darker, lower, and slower, describing dolor and deception, wandering and pain, rue and regret, the song, suffocated in nostalgia, drifted away, withered into a whisper, to a lost, tardy, and pointless cry.

Pantazi wiped his eyes.

"Ah," said Pirgu to Pașadia, making his eyes melancholy and voice sweet, "ah, this will be the waltz we play while I take you to your final resting place—as soon as possible. I doubt you will make me wait much longer for what will be the greatest celebration of my tender years. So beautiful it will be, so beautiful! Me, piss-drunk, with Mr. Pantazi, I will mop my collection of sad, warm tears, as I bid farewell, in a moving speech, to my eternally unforgotten friend."

Pașadia said nothing.

"Yes," Pirgu continued, swooning his voice and gaze even more, "so beautiful! I will place cordons and medals on a cushion beside you. And after seven years, when they dig you up again for your grand memorial, I'll wager they find you still elegant, crisp and well groomed, without a single gray hair, cured in mercury and rubbing alcohol like a pepper in salt and vinegar."

But Pașadia was not listening; his mind was elsewhere. Pirgu escaped this time, and I felt unlucky, since I did not have eyes to see him.

Alone in Bucharest from a young age, living on my own, I kept distant from the herds. The restricted circle of my acquaintances, those chosen few, would never have included Gorică Pirgu, if he were not the inseparable fellow of Pașadia, for whom I had a boundless devotion.

Paşadia was a brilliant star. A series of events had endowed him with one of the most complete formations possible to the human mind. I have been close to many of those considered our nation's most famous. Very few have I seen composed as splendidly by so many great gifts as this unjustly treated person, who, by his own will or his life's, had surrendered himself to oblivion. And I knew no other to have suffered the blind enmity of so many.

I heard this might be due, in part, to his appearance. Still, what a handsome head he had! And yet some renitency was there, something dormant and disturbing; so much bridled passion, such fiery arrogance and brutal animosity were contained in the contours of his torpid face, in the satiated pleats of his lips, the power of his nostrils, in those disquieting eyes beneath heavy lids. And what little he said, in a dull, labored voice, he spoke with bitterness, with deep revulsion.

His life, according to the story he seldom told, became a terrible struggle early on. Descended from people of prestige and station, he was abandoned at birth, raised by alien hands, and then exsputed to another country for his education. On his return, he saw himself dispossessed by his family, robbed, harassed, persecuted, and by everyone betrayed. What was not turned against him? With what strident injustice did forces gather, what unremitting industry to steal his youth, what exertion to bury him in silence! Through trials of every type, through many sorrowful years of struggle, any one of which would have toppled a giant, this iron being was doubly tempered. Paşadia was not a man for resentment; his self-confidence and cold blood never left him, even in his blackest moments. Steadfastly pursuing his goal, he faced down the hostility of his surroundings, he masterfully turned it to his own ends. Like none other, he knew to wait and be patient, obstinate he stalked opportunity, he clenched and clutched that which, under a normal course of events, should have fallen to him from the beginning, without trials and harrowing. Once arrived, he transcended all, surveyed his wondering foes, and, iron-fisted gelder with velvet gloves, he satisfied his desires. The pathways of the great opened to him, wide and smooth; yet now that he could dream of having everything, he no longer wanted anything, and he withdrew. I supposed the root of this strange decision was to some extent a fear of himself, since beneath the icy outer veil, Paşadia hid a passionate soul, complex, tenebrous, and which, despite his control, would betray itself in slips of cynicism. With the venom built up in his petrous heart, power could easily have made him dangerous. And he demonstrated that any belief in virtue, honesty, or good, any pity or indulgence for human weakness was, to him, completely foreign.

His withdrawal from politics was less of a surprise than the subsequent transformation in his way of life. At the age when others began a process of atonement, he, who had always served as a living example of elevated comportment, threw himself into debauchery. Was this the revelation of a life he had led, up to that moment, in darkness, or the rediscovery of an old practice, the craving for which made him disburden a long line of exemplary years?— because it was unnatural to shed such a skin overnight. Whether it was possible, I do not know, but regardless, I seldom happened upon a player that handsome, a rake that superb, or a drinker that grand. Could one say he had lowered himself? Not at all. With sober elegance, full of dignity in carriage and speech, he remained a European man-of-the-world to the tips of his fingernails. To preside over a grand congress or an academy, no other would be more fitting. One who did not know him, seeing him pass in the evening, robust and grave, trailed by a hansom, could never be made to imagine what base and nasty places that commanding gentleman would enter to drown himself until daybreak. For me, the tableau of his life contained something terrifying; I sensed that a dark spiritual drama unrolled within, whose mystery remained unpenetrated.

If, in trying to provide some sense of the features of this noble face, I have paused so long, it is because I did not want to miss the opportunity of bringing him to life again before my eyes, as dear as his memory is to me. In Paşadia, I met another man, wholly other than the peregrinator of dens of Bucharestean iniquity. But this person I encountered otherwhere. A few steps off of Podul Mogoşoaiei, along a lonely alley, in the shadow of an ancient, flowerless garden, an old house rises, dark and inhospitable. I was one of the few privileged to cross the threshold of that wealthy residence where every corner was touched by the austere soul of its master.

I would find him in his study, an abode of quiet and recollection, where nothing of the outside world could penetrate. In that chamber, lined with baize cloth, surrounded by wardrobes nailed to the walls and heavily curtained windows, how many unforgotten hours was I held, fixed in a high-backed chair, by the conversation of my host. Weighty and far-reaching, restrained and masterful, lacking elaborations, divagations, and pointless things, it gathered one within its powerful webs, it astonished, it ravished. Paşadia was additionally a master of the quill, and in his youth had painted well. The quantity of his reading was unbelievable. History he knew like no one else, its study had developed his inborn gift for judging people without mistake; for many, at that time at their height, he foresaw an imminent and tragic ruin, and I cannot forget how his eyes, as he spoke the fatidic words, flashed sinisterly. Paşadia Măgureanu! I took the man's sympathy for me like a gift of Providence, and I am proud to be the disciple of this great revolutionary, this stoic. For all the deficiencies the world found in him, I will not allow but one alone—and that one unforgiveable: his society with Gorică.

Gore Pirgu was a sack of slime without pair or peer. His uncouth humor, like a cheeky court-jester, earned him the reputation of being a clever boy, to which was added—why, no one knows—also that of being a good boy, although he was only good at being bad. This white clown had the soul of a dogcatcher and gravedigger. Spoiled to the marrow from a young age, cardsharp, crimper, maid-ruiner, running with the pimps and swindlers, he had been the Benjamin of the Cazes Café and the Cherubino of the whorehouses. It disgusted me to research in more detail the complications of this rotten, sad creature, one who felt an unhealthy attraction solely for the foul and the putrid. In Pirgu's blood ran the desire for the depraved, gypsy life of our past ages, for love affairs on the wrong side of town, shindigs at the convents, songs without decency, for anything one could call disgusting or shameless. He could only converse about the card-playing he plied as a trade and the scabbado that had enervated him prematurely; these were the complete foundation of the spirit with which he enchanted those who prized his idiocy. And yet, none other did Paşadia find to make his comrade, even though he, in contrast, scorned the superficial, belittling and ridiculing it mercilessly whenever he had the chance.

"Turn and look, if you please," Pașadia said to me, "don't let your neighbor commit suicide; look at him, he's swallowing his knife."

It was true; Gorica was zealously working his knife over a poorly cooked sturgeon, passing a piece through the mayonnaise, and, still with the knife, jabbing it into the back of his mouth. I pretended not to see, or hear. Pantazi bent to look for something under the table.

"The precepts," continued Pașadia, "of elementary good breeding state: neither the knife in fish or vegetables nor the fork in cheese, and, never in any way, the knife in the mouth. But this, this is for finer people, the prodigy of boyars, not for rubes, not the dregs. Who can teach a swine to drink from crystal?"

For Pirgu, who thought his knowledge of high society unequaled, no rebuke could have cut him more to the quick. He recovered quickly, however, and arrogantly told Pașadia he was at the point of writing him off.

"It's a good idea for you to cut me down with your manners and airs," he said haughtily, "because otherwise I'd bare my teeth. You've gotten old and demented . . ."

To make peace, Pantazi directed the waiter to uncork the champagne, which, following the custom of our meetings, was served in large glasses. Pirgu would only let one finger's worth be poured, on top of which he added almost a liter of soda water, some light Hungarian borviz. Of the four, he was the only one disinclined to drink; one could say he more pretended to drink, filling himself with spritzes of soda, blue soda. Still, he was seldom not drunk by morning, and when he was tipsy he would indulge in such antics that, had he a dram of self-consciousness, would embarrass him too much to meet anyone's eye.

Our low voices dedicating the cup to the health of Pantazi, our dear patron, we tasted the invigorating drink with delight. Pirgu only wet his lips and made a face.

"Champagne without dames," he pronounced, "isn't worth a dime."

Women had been, however, firmly and forever banished from our meals. All of Gorică's attempts to gain entrance for a girlfriend or two had been in vain. Pantazi would have agreed happily, but Pașadia was unbending. We limited ourselves to brief, prowling glances toward the ladies at neighboring tables, who, with some regularity, returned similarly evil-minded winks.

With his dark and turbulent stare, Pașadia undressed a plump Jewess seated a bit in front of him. I joined him in this Christian deed, knowing I would not bother my great friend in the least. Aware of her wonderful Eastern beauty in full flower, her matte face white like a wax doll, where velvet eyes burned a cold flame between silken lashes, she was unmovable, unimpressible, in the unbounded aloofness of a chosen people, just as her ancestors had been while they were dragged and stripped in slave markets, or hung, later, from their wrists by Torquemada. As she crossed one leg over the other, her dress rose above her knee, exposing, vaguely, through the transparence of black stockings, her lathe-smooth thighs. When she decided to cover them, it was without haste or blushing. Pirgu was shamelessly boring a merchant-lady, her face flushed beneath her make-up, puffy and bejeweled. Smiling sweetly, with eyes half-closed, he raised his glass, sipped delicately, then licked his lips with pleasure. Only Pantazi looked at no one. The dreamer as always, he stared into space, quiet and sad. He pointed for more champagne.

But Pirgu took things one joke too far. Holding his empty glass like a telescope, he blew kisses with the other hand to the body of the statuesque merchant-lady, who burst into laughter. Pașadia advised him to refrain from making trouble.

"Would you take it kindly," he asked, "to find yourself picked up and tossed out?"

Pirgu regarded him with scornful pity.

"Do you think that I am someone like you, a person who would be kicked out just like that, one-two, hugger-mugger? Is there anyone here who doesn't know me, or anyone anywhere, who doesn't love me, anywhere I can go where I'm not at home?" To prove his point, he stood up and went to the merchant-lady's table, kissed her hand and whispered in her ear, then took a turn around some other tables, stopping longest by the beautiful Jewess.

"Little Rachel has asked," he said on returning, "how one as refined as myself, the scion of boyars, could associate with such boring people? She was vicious. I begged her to take no notice; one, I said, is a poor, broken old man, he once was somebody, but now he's gone to seed; the other is a child." Paşadia swallowed and was silent. I followed his example. I did not hide my admiration for Pirgu's breadth of acquaintances. People of every variety and caliber, many people, all the people. Whom did he not know, truly, where had he not penetrated? Into the locked houses of merchants both frightened and frightening, the iron-barred enclaves of superalimented Jews, the claptrap nests of scabid scullery-maids, wherever he went, Gorică was greeted with open arms, if not always by the front door. It remains a wonder how nowhere did he inspire revulsion or fear, how no one would intuit in that prancing little mutt, wagging its tail and baring its teeth, its keen and clever enmity, endless, omnidirectional, the vile and rabid beast, ready to wound, betray, and prevaricate, seeming to serve only as destiny's tool of fraction and dissolution. Neither was his perniciousness shy to show itself, as he took pride in adventures for which the law would have awarded either jail or the mental asylum.

While at school, he led his friends to crab-ridden women. For these kinds of things he enjoyed an unstoppable, demonic imagination. The excitement of the orgy, to which he dedicated body and soul, became his apostolate. Skilled in panders and whoremongery, his beacon guided tender young men of ready money to ruin, and many more women to their downfall; thanks to him, famous names became tainted with improbity. Seldom did anything impure happen without his involvement, drawn only by his raw and insatiable appetite for cruel sport, for the sake of which nothing would give him pause: spying, defamation, gossip, vituperation, accusation, threatening to make public secrets confided or extracted, anonymous letters—all seemed the same to him, each to be used as needed. The question arose: what more could Gore Pirgu do to be known as a bad boy?

So gratified was Pirgu by my admiration, I didn't have to ask him twice to recount what had befallen Mrs. Mursă. But I was interrupted by little Rachel's departure. With supple steps, she neared our table to retrieve her mantle from a nearby hook. Pirgu leapt to help her. Rachel was at her best, a wonder; she recalled the comparison of women and flowers—a black flower, tropical, filled with poison and honey—engendered unintentionally by the warm scent rippling, dizzying and passionate, from each of her motions. Up close, however, without her beauty losing any of its allure, the lady was somehow repugnant. In her, more so than in other women, one sensed Eve, the irreconcilable and eternal feminine enemy, purveyor of temptation and death. Her quiet gaze, passing over our corner, produced a terrible spark when it collided with Pașadia's.

A callow fellow followed her, hunched and haggard, with circles around his glassy eyes and cheeks of an unhealthy ruddiness. He coughed dryly and suffered continuously. He took leave from Pirgu with a smile that seemed to hold the pain of eternal departure.

"That's Mișu," whispered Pirgu to us. "He has a foot in the grave, he's leaving us. She's finished this one off, too; two men in three years, not even counting the ones on the side. Brava, what an extraordinary woman, on my word of honor!" And then to Pașadia, "Tell me, if you're going to put your hat in, can you manage alone or do you need backup? Let me know and I'll give a word, it's in my area."

In place of a response, Pașadia drained his glass down to the last drop.

"If you had the chance, why would you think twice?" said Pirgu. "They'll be making your coliva soon enough. As if everyone doesn't know that the best you can hope for is licorice and jam. You're looking at the dregs, at least try to die happy . . ."

Suddenly a lively din broke out all over the restaurant. People got up from their tables and ran for the exits. Horns were heard, firemen passed. The young man serving us said it was nothing: a chimney had caught fire near Old Court Church, but it was out before the pumps arrived. Since some diners owned or rented houses near the place, everyone had taken alarm, thinking his home might be touched by the fire, so threatening in those narrow alleys, with houses one on top of the next.

Conversation turned to the Old Court, whose name, without the green-steepled church to carry it, would have been lost to memory. With his famous intelligence, Pașadia laid out almost all that was known about this residence of the rulers of old. Not much, as it seemed. Like the rest of the city, the Court had been razed and rebuilt numerous times. It must have once covered a wide area, as remains of its foundation extended throughout the circumjacent environs, beneath, for example, the restaurant where we sat. How the Court had looked was easy to imagine, resembling the monasteries in large part, a group of several buildings, made to house the polloi and Gypsies, without design, without style, cobbled from additions, plaster, and patches, ready to serve, in its ugliness, as backdrop to the miscreancy of powerful gangs culled from foreign cripples and heavily dosed with Gypsy blood.

I asked whether one should not look to the instability of rulers and a fear of invasions to explain why we had nothing so grand and long-lived as the West. The noble pleasure in construction was not lacking in some of the voivodes; Brâncoveanu, for example, raised wealthy courts on his extensive estates. Pașadia responded no; the love of the beautiful was a privilege enjoyed by peoples of exalted origins, a number in which our nation could not be included, as we had contributed nothing to civilization. He then cursed Brâncoveanu and knocked off his lordly cap, his mantle as prince of the Holy Empire, his capote as Magyar count, and his lance of Saint Andrei of Russia; in a few strokes Pașadia portrayed him as a glistening Gypsy king, a salesman and servant—the very soul of a slave. That he had been infected by the fad, imposed by the powerful of his time, for building, sowing, and ornament, this much was true, but from this wealthy barnacle, who reigned during the tumultuous flowering of the Baroque, what remained? He left us: the columns at Hurez, the arcade porch at Mogoșoaia, the palace at Potlogi, and what else?... these kinds of scrawny, odious remnants should make us proud? The whole story, once and for all, should be buried, as shameful as it is!

This outburst did not surprise us. Pașadia, observing and judging with unrelenting severity all that was Romanian, often took his obstinacy to the point of bad faith. The hatred that smoldered unasleep within him would swell and surround him, whirling, enormous, burning him like coals, buffeting him like a gale. Since it was not possible to challenge his claim, I found it pointless to rise in defense of that past, the mirage to which my quill owed a marvelous temple of icons, which in my youth I fretted over with an almost pious devotion. Nor was there any need, once Pașadia, on his own, revised his harsh pronouncements.

"It is strange, though," he admitted. "Although I find them less important as art than as history, I cannot deny these humble vestiges a peculiar charm. Before the least important of them, my imagination takes wing, I feel moved, deeply moved."

"I, for one, understand," said Pirgu, "because you're a ruin, too, a venerated ruin, not all that well preserved."

He laughed. This was how we behaved. The cult of Comus had brought us together, almost daily, for the past month, at lunch or supper. But the real pleasure came in our idle conversation, the palaver that embraced only the beautiful: travel, the arts, letters, history—history especially—gliding through the calm of academic heights, whence a joke of Pirgu's knocked it down into the mud. It was sad that a lack of culture kept this enemy of the printed word foreign to our discussion. In Pantazi, however, Pașadia found a clear mind, a fortified and free spirit; I was afraid to miss a word of their luminous exchange of views and bodies of knowledge, and the fact that they stayed with me, the remarks that I took care to record, consoled me, possibly even repaid me, for all the material losses I had suffered from the war until then.

To my great regret, that evening the fête would break up early; Pașadia was leaving for the mountains around midnight.

"I am anxious," he said, "for the day I return, so we can see each other again, at my house." And to Pirgu, "We'll have a little poker, no? You need the practice."

Pirgu was enflamed by a terrible rage, to abate which he loosed a quiet flood of vituperation, from horseman's jeers to grocer's insults to slop-maid's curses. We learned that before dinner, at the casino, Pașadia, who played against Pirgu with vehemence, had shaken every last coin out of him, in an epic contest. Pirgu had lost twenty-five pols and owed as many more.

In an effort to calm him, Pantazi asked if he needed money. Pirgu responded proudly to the negative, which surprised us, even after we saw him take a stack of hundreds from an envelope. He had played all night, at the Arnoteanus' house, near the tracks, and had replenished himself. Pașadia asked for his debt.

"None for you!" said Pirgu.

Pantazi paid our bill, with fat tips to the boys and musicians. We departed. But the hansom that awaited Pașadia, in the narrow alley in front of the restaurant, could not move, because of a crowd that churned, laughing and shouting, in front of us. In the midst of the group, screaming like a beast, a woman fought against three rigid officers, who could barely hold her down. When she practically fell into our arms, our quartet took one step in retreat.

Old and withered, dressed in rags, with her head unmantled and one foot bare, she seemed, in her terrible writhing, a creature of hell. Dead drunk, she had vomited on herself and lost control of her bladder, to the delight of the crazed gang of street punks and hookers that paraded beside her and shouted, "Pena! Pena Corcodușa!"

I noted that Pantazi startled and paled. But at the sight of us, a blind fury engulfed Corcodușa. What was given for us to hear would have shaken the most profane heart. Even Pirgu was left with his mouth hanging open.

"Listen well and commit it to memory," Pașadia whispered to him. "It's a good chance for you to complete your education."

The cavash moved the drunk woman along. Pantazi entered into conversation with a girl who, with enthusiastic brazenness, had watched with a smile the entire sad spectacle of human depravity. He asked her if she knew the terrible harridan that now had plopped onto the middle of the bridge, like a bear, and refused to stand.

"She's Pena Corcodușa," said the girl, "she's drunk again. When she's sober she's all right, but if she starts in, she gets ugly."

After he put something in her hand, Pantazi talked with the girl a little more. He learned that Pena lived by the Old Court, sat in the church by the candle table, and did odd jobs in the market. Her avocation and employment was to wash the dead. She had been, some time ago, in the nuthouse.

With great effort, the officers were able to lift her. When she found herself on her feet and again laid eyes on us, she started shouting, ready to resume da capo her friendly greeting, yet being too fast and brittle her voice was lost in babbling.

"You rakes," she was able to shout, "rakes of the Old Court!"

Was it someone else, from some other age, that spoke through her—who knows? But nothing else in the world, I think, could have given such pleasure to Pantazi as this antique expression, long fallen from use. His face lit up, he repeated it endlessly.

"It's true," admitted Pașadia, "one of the happiest combinations of words. It surpasses 'Knights of the Bronze Horse,' which has the same meaning, from the time of Louis XIII. There's something equestrian about it, something mystical. It would make a wonderful title for a book."

"Unhappy Pena," murmured Pantazi, melancholic, after a period of silence, "I never thought I would see you again. What memories!"

"You know her?" Pirgu asked, surprised.

"Yes, it's an old story. A love story, and not one you hear every day. It was around the War of Seventy-Seven. I doubt many women have lost the vivid memories that the Russians left them, women of every level. It was pure insanity. Over the beds, like a pestle into a mortar, rubles rained over a ravenous Danaë. In Bucharest, the Muscovites found their Capua. Our ladies only had eyes for Russian officers. But the man that drove everyone crazy was Leuchtenberg-Beauharnais, beautiful Sergei, the grandson of the tsar. Hopelessly, however, did they wait for him to lower the flag, because chance had thrown him, on the first night, into the arms of an ordinary woman, and from her arms he could not free himself. She was from the edge of town, not that young, gray along the temples. I knew her from masked dances in summer gardens. The charm of this being, unusually glum, more odd than pretty, lay in her eyes, a pair of large green eyes, cloudy green, sides-of-a-fish as the Romanian says, heavy-lashed and over-browed, with a drifting gaze. Did any other allurement weave the net that caught the duke? Possibly. Yet beyond any doubt, the two shared a passionate love, a flame between a lily of the town green and Prince Charming, whose being reflected, deep inside, the sparkle of a second royal wedding. It was agreed that, after the war, Pena would follow the lord and master to Russia. Lichtenberg departed to die like a crusader in the Balkans. I followed his body as far as the River Prut. In the evening of October 19, 1877, the funeral train passed through Bucharest, with one car transformed into an ardent chapel and mortuary where, among an abundance of torches and candles, priests in robes and honor guards in shining breastplates held vigil over the flower-covered reliquary of the hero, stopping only a few moments to receive honors. The crowd raised a piercing shout and a woman fell like a stone. You understand who it was. When she awoke, she had to be restrained. "Since then, thirty-three years have passed."

Pantazi put out his cigarette. The sorrowful story of Pena gave us no less pleasure than her estimable jibe did him. Pașadia bid farewell and climbed into the carriage.

"See you later, fornicator," yelled Pirgu.

Gorică now slurred and mixed up his words. It took him some effort to tell us that he had played like a priest; the late "Poker" himself wouldn't have played any better.

"Still, I folded," he whined. "I folded and got nothing. But he'll pay me back, and dearly, that Caiaphas, I'll clean him out."

He pressed us to go out with him.

"Come on, gentlemen," he insisted, "I won't steer you wrong." We asked him where he would take us.

"To the Arnoteanus," he responded, "the true Arnoteanus."

It was not the first time that Pirgu had offered to take us there. To get rid of him, we swore an oath to accompany him any other time but that evening. At the Mogoșoaia Bridge we separated, Pirgu going toward the post office, the rest of us toward Sărindar. The night was wet and cold, the fog thicker and thicker. I had just thought how much I would rather be at home, in bed, when Pantazi, as was his manner, asked me to sit with him. Was there any chance I would decline, that I could say it was his fault I was in no shape to stay out? If for Pașadia I felt devotion, then for Pantazi I felt weakness, one coming from the head, the other from the heart, and however hard one might try, the heart went before the head. This odd man was dear to me even before I met him. In him I felt I had a friend since the world began, and often, more than often, another version of myself.

The Three Peregrinations

C'est une belle chose, mon ami, que les voyages . . .

—Diderot

A friend since the world began, thus did he seem to me, even though before that year began—1910—I had never so much as imagined one like him existed in the world. He appeared in Bucharest along with the budding leaves. After that, I saw him always and everywhere.

His sighting had been a pleasure from the start; I had been seeking such an occasion for some time. There are creatures who, through some little thing, perhaps without us knowing precisely what, awaken a vibrant curiosity within us, stoking our imagination until we forge our stories around them. I have always reproached myself for the weakness I have toward beings like these; had I not paid dearly enough in my misadventure with Sir Aubrey de Vere? This time, however, grafted onto my curiosity was an overwhelming new sentiment: a spiritual affinity almost to the point of tenderness.

Could it have come from his charming sadness? Possibly, the dear man's eyes spoke so much. Somewhat sunken beneath the arch of his eyebrows, a rare blue, their line of sight, unspeakably sweet and veiled in nostalgia, seemed to follow the recollection of a dream.

They made this person strangely younger. In other ways they did not betray his age, they illumined his serene brow, they completed the noble features that formed the matte pallor of his dark face, drawn down by a pointed beard as soft as corn silk, the color of which it shared. Something of the same color was his usual costume, everything about him being muted, mellow, mollified—his gait, his manner, his speech. He was exhausted, or timid, or greatly proud. Ever alone, he progressed through his life in a state of self-effacement, desiring to lose himself in the multitudes; yet the mob and he were so mismatched that his external simplicity, evidently intended to have him pass unnoticed, had the opposite effect; it caught the eye so strongly that he seemed even more foreign. But foreign he was not. Neither, though, did he resemble Romanians: he spoke the language too beautifully, as he did French, even perhaps with a little more difficulty. We had often been seated at neighboring tables—today at one of the city's foremost eateries, tomorrow on some tavern's porch. I always felt grateful for his proximity, but in one place in particular his sadness resounded so deeply in me that he seemed another version of myself: in a park, Cişmegiu, the Cişmegiu of that time, lonely and left to its wildness.

Under the high trees, at dusk, the unknown man took his melancholy for a walk. He stepped with solemnity down the paths, leaning on a cherrywood cane, smoking, halted at times by his thoughts. But what could they be, that they overwhelmed him, that they moved him to tears?

The stars had already shone for some while when, without haste, the dreamer finally permitted himself to leave. He went to take dinner. Toward midnight he presented himself at an establishment where he stayed as late as possible, until closing. Then he would meander through alleyways, advigilating the impending dawn.

I said I saw him everywhere. I grew used to him; were there a day without, I felt the lack keenly. Spotting him once at the train station, as he took the Arad, I was overtaken by a childish panic that he was leaving for good, my unknown friend, the person whose gentle eyes regarded the sky, trees, flowers, children . . .

It would have been difficult to forget him, as his memory was so closely bound to Cişmegiu, and I remained faithful to the park, even during the great showers that fell in advance of the comet's appearance that summer. As the verdancy awoke toward evening, utterly inebriated with humidity and emptiness, the garden revealed its unimagined beauties. And in the most wonderful of all evenings, on the wide bridge over the lake, I had the pleasant surprise of re-encountering my friend.

Propped against the unsteady guardrail, he trained his gaze upon the brilliant, rising white of the morning star. Noting my burning cigarette, he approached to ask for a light, and this flame was enough to thaw whatever ice there was between us. I learned that I was not completely foreign to this man: we had met so often. He had only been waiting for the chance to introduce himself to me, and he thanked the surroundings that provided it, in this very night.

"Faced with Beauty," he explained, "solitude becomes a burden, and tonight is very beautiful, dear sir, a night out of a fable or a dream. This kind of night returns to us, so they say, from a long time past; out of their mystery the old masters liked to form sacred legends, yet only rarely did the quill of the sharpest of them succeed in describing the limpid shadow in all of its translucent blue. Tonight is the expulsion of Hagar, the flight into Egypt. It's as though time is fascinated and slows its gait. And the wet air suffers no breeze, the branches no murmur, the light on the water no shudder . . ."

Today, so many years later, I hear him still. His speech was measured and spare, lending even his most insignificant comments the charm of his solemn, warm voice, which he knew to modulate and inflect, to make it rise or fall with happy skill. I walked beside him; the pleasure of my listening grew in the shadows of that almost mystical night, its deep blue refracted in his eyes, and its endless quiet in his whole being; I listened without tiring for the whole night. But, for all he had to tell, a single night was not enough; on parting, toward morning, we agreed to meet the next night, which passed in the same way, and then again, and again, without interruption, one after another, for nearly three months . . .

. . . these, among the few pleasant months of my life. As the days grew shorter, we met earlier, parted later. Had there been no more day at all, and we stayed together without interruption, I would have had nothing to regret; with him, even eternity would be pleasant. Nothing was more monotonous, however, than the way we passed time. Our conversation prolonged supper almost to midnight; we continued speaking outside, calm peripatetics, up and down the wasted alleys of unknown peripheral areas, forgetting we were in Bucharest. Sometimes, reaching an open area, the man would stop to look long into the sky, which became more and more beautiful toward autumn and whose every constellation he knew. When the weather was bad, we went to his house.

He lived on the quiet Str. Modei, on the second story of a building owned by King Carol, with an elderly French woman who let him two chambers, richly furnished in the heavy style of fifty years ago, a salon in front and a bedroom in back, separated by a high partition built of window panes. Within the abundance of ebony and mahogany, of silks, of velvets and mirrors—beautiful, frameless, wide as the walls themselves—the tenant's love of flowers, impelled to obsession, produced a crazed harvest of roses and tulips, which, together with the candles we would find alight in both of the five-stemmed silver candelabra whenever we arrived, marked a select luxury, framing my host in such harmony with his being that my memory cannot disentangle his person from the place.

But then the enchantment was under way: the man spoke . . .

The narration undulated languidly, braiding a rich garland of noble literary blossoms from all peoples. Master of the craft of painting with words, he effortlessly found means to express, in a tongue whose familiarity he claimed to have lost, even the most slippery and uncertain forms of being, of time, of distance, such that the illusion was always complete. As though bespelled, I undertook long, imaginary journeys with him, journeys such as no dream ever provided . . . the man spoke. Before my eyes unrolled charming throngs of tangible visions.

Proud ruins ascended mountainous heights skirted in ivy; the venous verdancy suffocated the weathered fortress walls. Desolate palaces dozed in abandoned gardens, where stone gods, dressed in flesh, smiled as the autumn wind scattered mounds of rusted leaves, gardens with fountains where the waters no longer danced. The train of the full moon cascaded over old, sleeping cities, flashing fires caressed the swamps. Lavants of lights gilded the mud of enormous sleeping metropoleis, igniting bits of the fog above them like the pockmarks of disease. Away from their charcoal and beige we rapidly fled; at dawn, the snowcaps bled in the mist. We set to confront the peaks' bracing dizziness, leaving behind the flowering fields; we climbed through evergreen groves, tracing the whisper of brooks scattered beneath ferns; we climbed, inebriated by the potent air, higher, ever higher. Below our path, between bare scarps and arrizes crowned with thick pine trunks, the valleys extended along the snaking creeks that petered into the haze of thick, distant fields. A prolonged rustling rose like a prayer. In the peace of a limitless aloneness, we gazed in praise at the eagles' slow rotation over black cliffs, and at night we felt closer to the stars. But soon, a gale began and the temperatures plunged and toward midday we were compelled to descend, into crags with tender names where autumn languished until spring, where every suffering, even death, vested the face of voluptuousness. The bitter emanation of oleanders spread over sorrowful lakes that mirrored white steeples mixed among funereal cypresses. Pious peregrines, we entered castles of quiet and forgetting, to genuflect before Beauty, we wandered along inclined paths and grassy squares, we venerated august masterpieces in old palaces and churches, we penetrated the soul of the past by contemplating the sublimity of its vestiges. The ship slid slowly between the banks great Hellenes and Romans had praised; the pillars of ruined temples rose from nodes of laurel trees. A Greek woman smiled at us over a fence draped with jasmine, we haggled with Armeniac and Judaic merchants in bazaars, we drank sweet wine in smoky cabacks with mariners and belly dancers. We were dazed by the diverse bustle of crowded, sunbathed docks, the calm rocking of masts; we were charmed by the gentle silence of Turkish cemeteries, the white delight of eastern cities languishing like harem girls in the shadow of grand cypresses; we let the blue spell of the Mediterranean ravish us until, overwhelmed by the torpor of its enameled sky and overtaken by the Libyan wind, we sailed into the ocean. Toward midnight, out of the dance of humidity and light, an endless delectation emerged to our wondering view. The tilting rays gilded the dry hoariness, rent the brume threaded with all the hues of the rainbow, and composed, as never before or since, heavy blushes of sunset, transparent violets and grays in long summer evenings, a magical brilliance of boreal dawns over glacial dunes. We turned next toward the tropics—we dwelt among planters in the melancholy dream of Florida and the Greater Antilles; we penetrated, along the trail of "orchid hunters," the verdant dark of the sylvan Amazon sparkling with darting parrots. Nothing escaped our ravenous investigations; we discovered lost paradises on the expanse of the peaceful ocean, where, under novel constellations, we made the long crossing, we headed toward countries of violets, toward the cradle of ancient civilizations; we celebrated the coming of spring at Ise; we sank into the rites of perdition of Chinese and Indian nights; we shuddered through scented evenings on the Bangkok waters. The burning air mellowed the silver bells of the pagodas, turning over the silver of broad plibani leaves. We forgot Europe; all that we had once admired now seemed utterly stunted and dull. We re-embarked, over and over, in search of deeper horizons, older forests, more florid gardens, grander ruins. Our satisfaction came only when beauty or oddity made us believe we were in oneiric realms, yet whatever the wonder, whether created by the sport of being or by human effort, it would not hold us long and we again set forth, wandering somber environs and ravines of solitude; we avoided the tristour of barren wastes, the horror of fetid pools, to return as quickly as possible to the sea.

The sea . . .

It shone like a pond, mirroring, within the refuge of the coast's curved arms, the turquoise firmament and pearls of its clouds, blossoming like a field or sparkling like a swarm of bats, pale and weak or vivacious, verdant, and vigorous, frothing toward the sky whose daughter it is: of this he spoke with a pagan's devotion, his voice sank into a tremble even to mention the name, as though he had revealed a mystery or mouthed a prayer. To voice praise of this, the enormous power of the globe in motion, the matrix of all that lives, unchained and unbespoiled, human speech was never truly enough, and even the most famous poets blanched when they attempted songs to her. His thought lay within her as though on the bed of a shell, she echoed endlessly in his heart, the one passion of his life, he desired to discover her grave . . .

. . . he now fell silent, his gaze lost in nothingness. For the space of an hour, I had felt something heavy press my chest, squeeze my temples. This man, accustomed to the dash of wind from across the expanse and the salubrious scent of marine gale, feared open windows; he lived imbrumated with thick smoke, candied in heavy scents. Late at night, the candle flames petrified like thorns and, from time to time, there was the smothered pop of a falling rose petal.

It was not his only oddity. I was sometimes reminded of that young Englishman whose sad history I had composed. He also lined his travel tales with select historical details; he also demanded every corner of the realm or of the waves reveal all it had ever witnessed, enlacing the landscapes of today with visions of yesteryear. He liked to dream before the cliffs from which Sappho threw herself into the sea, and on the shore where Pompeii's pyre was raised. Here was the beautiful Inês assassinated, there the mad king died imprisoned. But while the vast landscapes painted in a word by Sir Aubrey were barren of human spirit, as though just after the flood, those of my new friend teemed with the peoples of the entire world, in picturesque dress: sheiks and pashas, emirs and khans, rajahs and mandarins, priests and monks of all orders and sects, astrologers, hermits, wizards, bloodletters, leaders of wild tribes whose wedding guest he had been or party to a hunt, and he had suited their desires and tastes as much as he did those of his numerous European friends, with his natural courtesy—quiet, quaint, permissive, lacking pretension or prejudice of rank, unforced—that betrayed a great boyar in the highest sense of the word, one of the last of those who preserved what was pleasing and attractive in "the old regime." And I didn't ask myself who this Pantazi was—it appeared this was his name—this gentleman who craved the Beautiful and imbibed of the spring of all knowledge, who read Cervantes and Camões in the original and spoke Gypsy with beggars, this knight St. George of Russia; rather I resented, in this person so spoiled by fate, his predilection for sadness, the mystery of that quiet melancholy that enshadowed his being, romantically and endlessly mirrored in the sight of so many skies, so many seas and seashores. Bit by bit, their evocation awakened a new spirit in me, a nomadic, nostalgia-rent spirit; it ignited my desire to depart, the temptation of journeys toward the unknown, the charm of distant roaming, and made me tremble; and at the thought that I might remain the slave of a single speck of earth, be damned to macerate and minish unsatisfied and restricted, I suffered terribly —I felt beaten, pestled, and hopeless. Like those magical spears that alone could salve the wounds they made, only my strange friend's stories could mollify this evil drive, thanks to which I was lost in the world of dreams, drugged as though by poppies or cannabis, my imagination inflamed to match his own, and followed by no less bitter awakenings.

I had bound myself again to an unknown person in friendship, a bosom friendship; we were always together, his house was open to me at any hour; in the end, I stayed more at his than at mine. With autumn, he went out less frequently—he chilled easily; if the weather was bad, he would leave his curtains closed all day and keep his candles lit. He would speak longingly of a villa that waited for him, somewhere under a warm sky, at the edge of the sea, surrounded with greenery and flowers. Flowers—how he loved them! The last roses in Bucharest scattered their petals inside his house, and since the stems that took their place had no smell, handfuls of spiral vanilla poured forth their aroma from broad cups. Low tables offered you bonbons, raisins, and sugared beverages. The man lived within a boundless absence of care, nothing and no one bothered him; sunk among cushions, he smoked and narrated, new stories always followed by long lapses into thought, when his eyes welled up with tears. And aside from myself, I knew of no other guest.

But then, about one month before the night which began the present story, in the French estaminet where they religiously kept a table for Mr. Pantazi, in the most sheltered corner, there was at the supper-hour a ruckus. With what occasion the squawking assembly of Bucharest's most frou-frou entered the narrow room, I do not recall; I know only that, instantly sated with this dull and vacant people, I had decided to keep my eyes on my plate, when there was an entrance that deserved not to be overlooked. For a moment I imagined I saw, making use of the idiotic mob of social buffalo, two famished beasts enter a pen.

It was one of those close couples, usually born of perversion, who are so intertwined that you can't imagine either one alone. It was obviously vice that bound this duumvirate—what else could unite two such different men? The older one, with blackened hair, was hopelessly well-attired; his stiff but still svelte body wore a head such as our time would never trouble itself to create, and his severe face seemed to have returned from another era, its haughty features stained by revulsion and hatred. The other was much younger, flabby and flaccid; he rocked on legs that bowed around a projected belly; his grinning snout mirrored the filthiest indignity. The first, very cold, turned his melancholic gaze over the heads of the crowd, while the second's lively patchwork eyes played restlessly, gleaming with base ill will. The overall impression the second one gave was to his miscredit, yet when placed alongside the proud man, his shameless, low-life mug became even more repulsive.

"You couldn't find water at the bottom of a river," he shouted, loud enough for us to hear. "It's me, poor little Pirgu!" He shook Pantazi's hand familiarly and, avoiding mine, sat at our table without asking permission. His companion, however, only sat when invited and after the necessary presentations, which I performed with even greater pleasure as I had long desired to bring these two creatures together, Paşadia and Pantazi, meant to understand and to prize one another.

We kept the place open until daylight. Pirgu left and came back many times, ever drunker. To prove to Pantazi how much he loved him, he constantly called him "nene" and kissed him. "Don't let me kiss him, my brothers," he begged us, "I'll dispatch him to Govora." "Abject buffoon," Paşadia remonstrated, "mind we don't send you to Mărcuţa!"

It would have been fitting at that moment for all three of us to accompany him to the asylum; we would never be released. Did Pantazi and I not follow Paşadia in his nightlife, he who let himself be blindly led by Pirgu? An unimaginable world was unveiled to me, with depravities I would never have witnessed otherwise, and if I had heard tell from someone else, I would have thought them pure invention. Bucharest had remained faithful to its old norms of decrepitude; every step reminded us we were at the gates of the Orient. And yet, the debauchery surprised me less than the madness that dominated at every turn; I admit I did not expect to see so much and such varied freakishness fermenting, to encounter outbreaks of unbridled insanity. I could find almost no one who, sooner or later, did not betray some infirmity, who would not unexpectedly spout nonsense; I lost, in the end, all hope of meeting, in flesh and blood, a human creature completely sound of mind. The number of truly interesting cases remained, however, low, and among them, the only one I reckoned worthy of research was Paşadia.

I have already recounted how, some fifteen years earlier, my great friend had resolved a long struggle with the misorder of his melancholy zodiac and then had buried himself alive. Since that time, everything he did was so exaggerated and abnormal that you had to adopt the popular opinion: he was crazy. This was the person who, as part of the unhealthy perenmity he nurtured against Romania, had vowed to alienate himself forever as soon as his meager means would permit him, yet he came to emburse his coffers more than he had ever hoped, and then not only had he not crossed the border but established himself precisely in Bucharest, in the damned city, that place that overflowed with bitter memories. From one of Zinca Mamonoaia's old houses, acquired in liquidation, he made himself a sumptuous hermitage, completely restoring it and packing it with all kinds of rare valuables, where he lived grandly, like a boyar. How he lived was a tale of Halima: there was no house like his. He, who for fifteen years employed a chef and valet, did not take his meal until evening and then only at the bistro and, also for some time, never slept at home, in his own bed. He would not suffer his domestics, who emerged to fulfill his wishes and vanished mute as ghosts, to live under the same roof with him; they dwelt serenely in a building apart, where they coupled and spawned families and hangers-on of whom the master knew not a thing; there was a famous tale of the day he looked out through his window to see a long box being drawn out of his courtyard, and never did he ask the identity of the dead man. Because a list of all the oddities of this type would never find its end, I will content myself to name the most amazing: Paşadia lived, in alternation, two lives.

From morning to evening he did not leave his house, he did not get up from his desk, his books and papers; he read and wrote without pause. During this time he did not smoke, he only sipped from a strong cup of coffee without sugar. I would visit him occasionally, and each time was a celebration for me. What a select being, what a difference between this dear man and others, what a chasm! All the consecrated vulgarity usually practiced on this planet had left not even a shadow on him, no trace—nothing Balkan, nothing gypsy; crossing his threshold you crossed a border, you came to civilization. There dominated the ponderous delectations of the spirit. How then was it possible that this man of letters and the Court, who would have enriched the days of Weimar, should permit himself to partake, all night through morning, in the filthiness of a Pirgu, that this Occidental, fine in his tastes and particular in his manners, should ingest pastrami and unfiltered wine, tripe soup and fruit brandy—as though an old man of Vienna, lost in the spell of Mozartian dreams, would listen to Oriental jamborees? Had his will to live fallen quiet, had he become the blameless victim of a strange derangement? I thought so, and I doubt another interpretation would appear more plausible to whoever knew of the horrible inheritance that so emburdened Paşadia.

An age has passed since the first one with this name—to which was added the compellative Măgureanu, after a parcel of land afforded to the family by a baron—escaping some place in Turkish parts, to eschew punition for a double murder, resorted to Wallachia and became a local strongman. A sad fame survived the bloodstained man, who no one ever saw laugh. This unbeknown tramontane, rumored to have concealed his origins because they were too base, gave every evidence of the contrary, in body and soul; he demonstrated the signs of a lofty stirp in decay: orgulous carriage and noble shape, haughtiness, acerbity and cruelty, laziness, distain for his own life, thirst for revenge and a will to hate, traits that passed to his descendants who, had they not been constantly at odds among themselves, could have established a strong and fabled house. Not without foundation did some believe their choice of Wallachia was unpropitious, even though it was his line's passionate and recalcitrant nature, irritated by enmity, and not solely the animosity of their surroundings, that prevented them from reaching that level their valuable mental gifts intended. They showed themselves greedy for learning, pleasant in conversation, and masters of literature; quick-witted and competent, but without continuity in what they did, quirky and capricious, each carrying within him the germ of his own perishment and perdition, and if one considered the fate of the Pașadia-Măgureanu line, one would say that this people was burdened by a dark anathema that drove them without cessation toward extinction, while first supposing them to the most difficult ordeals of despondency. Uprooted and transplanted in foreign soil, the old stem, battered by enmity, pathetically scattered its last leaves. The murderous and torturous strongman fell early (poisoned, they say, by one of his own); the second, the cavalry commander, a hardhearted hunter, passed most of his life in the dark forests of Vlăsia; when accused of highway robbery and stamping false coins, he disappeared forever without his name being heard again; his son, the father of my friend, a father not worth the name, an enemy, an addict of card games, a rake and a drunk, macerated each installment of his inheritance and died in the throes of insanity. His cousin, a young poet, died in the same way; of the girls, the only one to be betrothed caught her hair on a candle the night of her wedding and burned herself alive. The women who mothered this people—the staid and hately Greek with clenched teeth hatching her long fury among crates of clementines and Gaza oranges, the enemious and daring Serbian who, on her deathbed, spit the communion wafer into the priest's beard and spent out her breath in curses on her children, the infest and hypocritical Brașovan who was consumed by cancer and envy—further envenomed that sickly bloodline, spawning a funereal dowry of mauvacity and improbity, but at the same time, each woman sharpened the wits of her round of offspring, that sterile wit, an ill will, to a higher level of acuteness. The souls of his predecessors nested unpeacefully within him, glinting in his somber gaze, grinning in his sinister smile, they stunted his rise, they blocked him from glory, they impeded his wondrous acquisition of achievements; and he alone knew how many times he must set all his self-control against them, an internal struggle more devastating than that against external malificence, and from which he did not emerge the victor, until the very end. One day, his watershed day, he let his predecessors reclaim a part of his rights, he himself lifted the bar, and then he plunged into debauchery, until he reached the bottom, yet, as I feel I must repeat, the degradation did not mark him for a moment, because if the patrician spends a night in Suburra, he does not change his manner, nor does he hide his rank, he is just as grand in his vices as in his virtues. Something unnatural happened that evening: such a strange numbness overtook him that the person Pirgu clung to, unopposed, did not seem Paşadia himself, but only his body; only his gaze remained alive, darker and more troubled, as evidence of a rending pain inside. He would sit, smoking cigarette after cigarette, sipping glass after glass, the entire night. I knew how to resurrect him; suddenly the man would revive, his eyes would clear, a cold, sad smile would illumine his lifeless face. I would turn conversation toward the times of yesteryear, of long ago. I knew that the vision of the past, his passion, was the only thing capable of moving him; he spoke of the past with a mystical recollection; the heresy that his shadowy and old soul might once have had other incarnations was the only sin he permitted his belief, the only gentleness and only caress. So strong was this vision for the man that he would immediately share it with us—with Pantazi and me. Then a new journey began, no less beguiling, a journey into centuries past. We would usually find ourselves in a century dear to us, and in all senses nostalgic: the eighteenth.

We three were progeny of renowned dynasts, a trio of knight-monks from the sect of Saint John of Jerusalem, called Maltese, proudly wearing on our chests the crown and white enamel cross hung on a ribbon of black canvas. We arose from the mists of the Rakish-Sun, raised by Jesuit fathers and armed by the Villenese. While young, serving in a naval caravan, we had sunk Barbary Tartars with a broadside; later we had fought on dry land for the triumph of the fleur-de-lis; we had been at Kehl with Berwick and with de Coigny at Guastalla; after that victory, we took our leave of military life and, yearning to see and to know, we, the unbroken trinary, embarked on a restless wandering, in the footsteps of Peterborough. Select courtiers, from one end of Europe to the other there was no court we did not investigate, our red heels echoed over all of their staircases, each one's mirrors returned our stalwart faces and inscrutable smiles; we cut our swath through court after court; well received and well regarded by all, we were guests of the Grand, the Holy, and the Illustrious, of great Conquerors, of the middling and small, the Abbess-Princesses, the Prince-Hegumens and the Prince-Bishops; at Belém and Granja, at Favorita and at Caserta, at Versailles, Chantilly, and at Sceaux, Windsor, Amalienborg, Nymphenburg and Herrenhausen, Schönbrunn and Sans-souci, at Haga-on-Maelar, the Hermitage and Peterhof—we were connoisseurs of "the sweetness of life." During the uninterrupted day- and night-long celebrations, we experienced what no other had or ever would, we indulged insatiably in all the delights of the senses and the mind, because, although lacking greatness, it was a blessed age, the last age of good pleasure and good taste, in short, the age of France, and above all the age of delectation, when even the churches replaced cherubim with cupidons, when, torpid with longing, hearts were presented in sacrifice to the blindfolded god, and we who had seen le Bien-Aimé throwing himself at the feet of the Marquise, had seen the philosopher of Potsdam moaning after Kayserlinck and saw Semiramis the Muscovite tearing out her hair over the death of Lanskoi, even we did not escape the sweet disease—"it was so beautiful at night under the high chestnut trees"—seeing in women not only an end but a means; since politics tempted us, we often made bedrooms into bridges; and because all of our work came to a happy end, we lived in the company of the chosen and served the satraps personally. Implicated, in the shadows behind every scheme and intrigue, there was no fabricking or unfabricking without us, our flattery and gifts purchased royal concubines and imperial paramours, we were advisors and guides to dignitaries, we worked behind scenes for their rise or overthrow, we fulfilled missions of all types: we allied with Belle-Isle at Frankfurt on the vote for Emperor, we accompanied Richelieu to make his petition in Dresden, we procured Watteau canvases in Paris for Frederic the Great, we carried the diamond jewels of Elizabeth Petrovna to be polished in Amsterdam, we ordered lace in Mechelen for Brühl—none of this came from the pursuit of wealth or glory, but only from our need to be constantly in motion, our restlessness. Insatiable rovers, eternally under way, passionately curious and pining for pleasure, we frenetically spent our souls in the tumult of the greatest era ever known; we shared in all of its enthusiasms and confusions. And we were mad for music, we campaigned for Rameau and for Gluck, and like three Rakes from the East, we knelt before the child that would be Mozart; we had a weakness for adventurers: Neuhoff, Bonneval, Cantacuzène, Tarakhanova, the Duchess of Kingston, the Chevalier d'Éon, Zannowich, Trenck—they all enjoyed our support, either hidden or public; we housed the old and depressed Casanova with Waldstein at Dux; we were attracted as well by all that seemed supernatural: the mirror of St. Germain, the carafe of Cagliostro, the *baquet* of Mesmer, the bizarrities of Swedenborg and Schröpfer found with us, who no longer believed in anything, credence. And we paid close attention to the works of Scheele and Lavoisier. Slowly, we built friendships with most of the people whose names history cannot help but emphasize, they sent us missives, they called us to make detours to Montbard or Ferney; we prolonged our charming stopovers with Hoditz, in the Silezian Arcadia at Rosswalde, we energized the retinue of the Empress in Tauris, we let ourselves loose in the frenzy of Venice Carnival, and still wearing masks, in the other Venice at midnight, our arms received the falling King, gunned down by Anckarström. It was written that the most beautiful of ages would close in blood, and when, after a few months, we saw between flashes of Phrygian caps a pale bearing on its end the head of the Lady of Lamballe, we understood that our time had passed as well, and because all that we had loved in the world would soon be crushed and ravaged and obliterated, we covered our faces and disappeared forever.

"Come off it, nene, enough with these hookah farts," a yawny Pirgu interrupted, "let's talk about women."

We had expected him to turn testy. Pașadia controverted Pirgu's claims to any sort of understanding of the gentler sex. With no less obstinacy, Pirgu sustained that as far as ladies go, Pașadia was a zero. To judge by the women Pirgu procured for Pașadia, anyone would share the latter view: nothing but venomous, stray and broken animals, the spoiled and the scrofulous—truly putrid. But why then did Pașadia, who with the money he had could pay for the earliest fruit on the market, satisfy himself with these women, enabling Pirgu, and taste was the last thing that man had, to make him a laughingstock? Like an old bloodhound, Gorică scavenged the edges of town, trolling for worthy girls to serve his model of beauty; he baited them with the image of wealthy, easy lives; with fatherly care he helped them take their first steps on the path of vice, and like a real father, he never touched them. His taste was completely different. His sensibility, which was repulsed by all that was clean and pure, only awoke when he was drunk, and then he needed women who were deformed, toothless, scolioic or distended, especially those who were fat and fleshy beyond measure, corpulent and encorsive, breaking the market scale, well-packed, bouksome and gross. And coming upon these disgustful women he would speak so foully that even pigs and monkeys, if they could have understood him, would have blushed.

"Don't spit," he grinned, "or you'll lose the taste. What do you want from a sick guy like me, to foam at the mouth?"

Things between them had just simmered down, when out of nowhere, another round of argument broke out. Pașadia never missed a chance to throw shade on anything Romanian. Pantazi always took his side, but without the same enthusiasm; for the one, it voiced his venom toward those creatures who had betrayed his love, for the other, only condescension toward an impoverished family member. In contrast, Pirgu's patriotism amazed even himself. I will never forget how, picking him up once from a meeting of parvenus in national dress, none of whom spoke a speck of Romanian, I had to cross myself when I spied him, a gentle shepherd of the Carpathians, his pan flute tucked into his waistband, dancing a hora with Papura Jilava. Rather than hear his poor native land calumnized, he preferred usually to absent himself, to rise and leave us, but only momentarily, as he always came back, and never alone. His company would sidle up, without asking our blessing, right to our table, and thus in less than a month I attended a parade of all of Bucharest's most impertinent, saugrenu, preposterous, disrespected—the dregs, the leprous, the residuum of society. Lost, as always, in the fog of his dreams, Pantazi did not take notice. I questioned why Pașadia, the deignous gentleman, did not reject them, in fact he did the opposite: he toasted them, he gave them his hand; and with some deftly phrased questions, he betrayed the fact that he was not so foreign to their world as his airs would lead one to believe. He would even take flame and sing, "Ah, running after soldiers, the infantry, the cannoniers . . ." Arm in arm did Pirgu lead Poponel to our table.

Under this nickname a regrettable person from the Ministry of Foreign Affairs made himself known, a young man with a great future, who like many others in his circle, showed a particular bent for certain unmentionable methods of a controversial school. Lamsdorf, Eulenburg, Metschersky were his spiritual fathers, and Poponel consistently enjoyed similar protectors and connections. At that time, the city had not been flooded with page-boys, so Poponel passed as uncommon. In his constitution, with a handsomeness that left nothing to be desired, stoked by all the flames of Sodom, lay the soul of a woman, the soul of one of those smelly servants who hang around the barracks at night. I will not remain on him much longer, to describe him would mean dipping my quill in filth and swamp water, and thus occupied I would profane not only the quill, but also the filth and the swamp. But still, his was not the blame: that belonged to God. At the diplomat's coming, Pașadia fell back into his somber torpidness and waited for him to leave, so he could re-address Pirgu with new and more acerbic imputations.

"How long," this man responded, "will you keep up these prejudices, how long? Why this persecution? Perhaps you want him to ask for your hand? No? Then what's your problem? Don't you rent your Russian coachman by the month?—let him rent his Turk. Do you ask anyone's permission to run around with hookers and sluts?—why can't he run with pretty men, with rakes?"

"Fine," declared Pașadia, "but why does he have to play the nanny?"

"Well, otherwise," explained Pirgu, "they're not nursing him."

He was a godforsaken trickster, a devilish shit. Ah! if he had wanted to—with his gift for broad, cheap sarcasm, his lack of culture or high ideals, his minute knowledge of the world of thugs, pimps,

and con-men, ruined maids, whores, and hurdy-gurdies, of the depraved and their speech—without much effort, Pirgu could have become one of the foremost authors of his nation; he would be known
as "maestro," showered with statues and given a state funeral. What
"sketches" he could have produced, dear mother of God! Let him
give voice to the hubbub of the elections and the slums. Perhaps
showing some proper restraint, the dear man was satisfied with ma-
nipulating events, pulling strings and remaining in the shadows. It
was a minor miracle the way he tangled and reversed things, how he
confused the small and made the great look dumb, all while he went
scot free; he could pull the wool over the whole town—and us too,
were the three of us anything more than his crèche figurines, dolls
he disposed of one after another, yanked up, tossed out, without
worrying if they shattered or broke? A more dangerous and dirtier dog than him you could not find, and no better guide for the
third journey we made, almost every night, the journey in life as it
is lived, not dreamed. Yet how often did I believe I truly was in the
midst of a dream.

The meal had just been completed and Pirgu wanted to weigh an-
chor. The man was thirsty. At that time, thank the Lord, one could
find inexpensive wines from Bordeaux and Bourgogne, good
enough for a royal banquet. But these were not precisely Gorică's
taste; he wanted a lighter wine, an indigenous wine, a backyard
wine; he had dredged up some terrifying bottles, from who knows
what corner of the slums, some clouded, moldy swill to poison us.
Like a true sea-dog, Pantazi would drink whatever was put in his
mouth, while Pașadia preferred noise, light, crowds. We left there
and tried another varietal; Gore was thinking of some wild moon-
shine, on someone's high porch, or some rabbit-blood, enough to
make you beat dogs with your hat. In between bars, we stopped for
a coffee at Proțăpeasca or Pepi Șmaroț and had a drink and a chat
with the girls, just long enough for Pirgu to set up Pașadia (or someone else) with a date the next day. We might stop a bit at the "club,"
where Pașadia would win a few rounds of chemin-de-fer, quickly,
without sitting down; we did this infrequently, though, since
women and cards were meant for the anteprandial hours. The party

began for real at the third stop, where we played for keeps. Around us the city's sinister noctambulant beasts mobbed and swarmed. Gorică felt at home with them, gave himself rein. Like mercury, he slipped from table to table, stirring up chortles and guffaws, heating the night up around him; he told the band what to play, bought them drinks, kissed their mouths, then battered them with insults and fists. As always, he gave up the field of battle toward morning. Foreign to the wildly increasing clamor, Pantazi and Pașadia bore mute witness, as though they were a thousand leagues away, while it seemed that precisely their own silence troubled them. And another strange thing: if Pirgu did not come—he might have had to dance for his dinner, or he was hung up in a card game with the palace scribe—then, even if we went to the same places, we would find ourselves nodding off over our drinks, everything seemed pallid and lifeless, all that spirited nightlife being just him, him, the living incarnation of excremental Bucharest. So we followed him without objection; with this dear man through snowy rain we trudged down the swampy, unpaved and unnamed streets on the edge of town, through vacant lots full of trash and animal carcasses, we practically had to crawl into the torporous humidity of short hovels, with dirt floors and low benches, as recently painted as the Gypsy girls, who, barefoot in red or yellow sack dresses tied with a rag below the knee, offered themselves to butchers and slaughterhouse workers for a dram of rachiu or a packet of tobacco. And even though we had not started with good families, we managed to go even lower . . . Then we ate tripe soup in the piața, and waited for dawn to pour over us.

Dawn . . .

. . . Pașadia frowned and shook himself, as though waking from a bad dream. I avoided his clenched face, that cloudy gaze whose terror no words could match. This must have been the same face worn—as he hurried back, his heart in his throat, fearful the light of day would fall across his path—by his ancestral murderer. Finally, we parted; each person vectitated his own cadaver in a separate direction: Pașadia and Pantazi went directly home, I to a sauna, Pirgu to his baba to be massaged with rose-petal vinegar and opodeldoc. His inquinations, whatever form they took, had come to seem so natural that in Jarcaleți, where he lived with his parents, his slum-bound neighbors no longer marveled when they saw him arrive in the morning with two floozies each singing a different song, with a bear, with Gypsy bands or paparudas, on the water-truck, on a stretcher, or in a hearse.

But our deturpation in the sad life of festivity produced at least one happy result. Within a short time, a noble friendship bonded Pantazi and Pașadia. I believe sincerely that their approximation was due less to their shared interests and courtliess than to their common sadness, even though the feeling for one was as blue and calm as those nights, they say, that return from ages past, while for the other it was a black and bottomless Gehenna. Since Pantazi most always shouldered these nocturnal expenditures, and in such a way that did not permit Pașadia to object, this man decided to host him in turn, not at the tavern, but at his house. For the first time, the Dutch tablecloths were taken from the buffets and chests, likewise the plates and Bohemian crystal, the silver inlaid with gold. The sumptuous sitting room flowered with yellow roses, waxy translucencies in the gentle amber light of those sweet autumn days, the beautiful remains of the year. I felt so far from Bucharest that I imagined that meal must mark the celebration of Pașadia's return from a long divagation, of his disburdening of Pirgu.

Although he had been invited, that man did not come. After the meal, we passed into a room of the most precious Viennese Rococo, everything, the walls and the furniture, dressed in saffron silks with silver adornments in the shape of lilies—the Kaunitz Salon, as we called it, because it was decorated with a sumptuous portrait of the Prince-Chancellor in his Golden Fleece mantle and modeled after one of the reception halls of his old Gartenpalast, on Mariahilferstrasse. Pașadia seemed made to live in this aristocratic décor, which fit his being and his soul so well, the scholar and thinker grafted onto a vomitous parvenu, who would reveal, to the degree he felt he was with his own type, all his abjection. Mute with wonder, Pantazi did not tire of admiring the man's noble dignity, his severe mastery over his movements and speech, the brilliant gale of that lively, bitter sarcasm, colder than frost, more cutting than steel, more venomous than wolfbane. I still cannot comprehend how he

could acquire these traits, since if it is true that, needing ages to de-
velop, a tradition remains the appanage of blood, where did that
drop come from, so blue and pure, which, rejecting the vice of laurels, flowered in his unexpectedly orgulous nature; what mysterious
family connections bound him to those illustrious dignitaries of the
past, with whose faces he surrounded himself and with whose rel-
ics, manners, and taste he was slathered, such that if these people
were reanimated, they would recognize themselves in him before
they would one of their own decedents? Then I understood why
they had yelled "raca" at him, I realized how monstrous he must
have appeared and strange to those former slaves and rascals who
attacked and tried to rend and destroy him.

As the night settled and conversation waned, all I had heard
about Pașadia pressed itself into my mind. There had been plenty of
nonsense said about him! His abrupt change from shining poverty
to red-hot wealth fired people's imaginations, even after so many
years: some say he was in the service of a foreign power, others that
he had knowledge of matters of gravity and his silence had been
dearly purchased—similarly, aside from these houses in which he
had invested heaps of money, no one knew of another holding anywhere under the sun, no source of income, and neither was he the
chief of a bandit gang or a coiner like his grandfather; or whatever
else one might conjure. They said his prosperity came from the old
strongman. Having reached advanced old age, very rich and very
alone, this man, sensing that the end was coming near, was said to
have called his grandson to him, from the far-off country where he
lived under an assumed name, and made him his heir. It was true
that the confused chronicle of my friend's life was missing a few
pages; for years on end he had lived in hiding, no one saw him, everyone thought he was dead. The mystery he always enjoyed gave
rise to another round of rumors: one heard tell, for example, that in
his locked house, surrounded by gardens, he was hiding, or holding, a woman, one not quite in her right mind; sometimes at night,
faintly, from one part of the house, came her screams. A story in the
back of the newspaper—the suicide, under unusual circumstances,
of a well-known Bucharest personality, whose wife, they said, had
maintained culpable relations with Pașadia—brought calumniation

to its climax: it was murmured that, when caught in the act and cornered, Pașadia did not hesitate to add, to the chain of his family's lawlessness, a link made of blood. Stories like these, even if they were woven with the warp of truth, did not interest me excessively; something else goaded my curiosity, precisely that which everyone else had failed to notice . On a regular basis, Pașadia would say he was going to spend a few days in the mountains, but the name of that mysterious Horeb, whence he returned with his powers refreshed, no one knew nor asked. It would have been natural to suppose that this steely being, who for weeks on end would sleep at most two out of twenty-four hours, and not in his own bed, found peace and rest in the profound solitude of balsamic altitudes, and I would have contributed this jot to the gossip, if from long ago, as a child, I had not heard my aunt tell of an old woman, related in some way to Pașadia, who said he occasionally suffered from manias, terrible "fits," but when he felt them coming on, he would lock himself up and stay hidden until they passed. These points became connected in my head, and I could not think of them without trembling.

Leaving with Pantazi, I found it strange for the first time that this man, who had seemed a friend to me since the world began and sometimes even another version of myself, had not even told me his real name: on the crowned monogram that marked some of his belongings, the first letter, from the name under which he was known, was missing. I was far from unsatisfied, however; to the pleasure of friendship with these unique creatures was added that, for me priceless, pleasure of standing in-between two mysteries, like two mirrors put face to face, two endless depths. I wondered only whether, one day, anything more of these mysteries would be revealed.

Confessions

... sage citoyen du vaste univers.

—La Fontaine

Pirgu set off toward the post office, we toward Sărindar. The fog grew thicker, the damp more penetrating. We entered the closest establishment, Durieu's, behind the National Bank, and selected a table in the back, in the most secluded corner. But that night, my friend was not himself: he did not tell stories, drink, or smoke. He only sighed occasionally and dabbed at his eyes. After the strange happiness of not even an hour ago, engendered by Pena's no less strange oracle, he had fallen into a sadness that was strange as well. I had never seen him in such dismay before now. I surveiled him discreetly, knowing that in such moments, relief comes from revelation, and I sensed something like was not far off. Nor was I mistaken: as soon as he had gathered himself somewhat, his hesitant voice began:

"I owe you an explanation, my friend. Perhaps it hasn't bothered you that, before this moment, I haven't told you who I am, but please, forgive me; it was not by design. For your sake, for all the friendship you have shown me, I wanted, from the very start, to give up the incognito I have adopted for the time I am forced to pass here; and if I have yet to do so, I simply have not had the occasion. We had so many other stories to tell! With you I have had the pleasure to relive thirty years of travel; and tonight, also with you, if you won't be too bored, I will relive my childhood and first youth.

"For this we will return to Bucharest, because in my own way I come from this city; I first saw the light of day on Podul-de-pământ, in my family's house on Viişoară. But I am an odd varietal." And here, suddenly gaining strength, his voice shone with a certain pride.

"I am Greek," he continued, "and noble, Mediterranean; my earliest ancestors, as far back as I know, were seafaring thieves, free and daring men, they ventured after prey far and wide across the waters, from Jaffa to Baleare, from Ragusa to Tripoli. The two branches of my family stem from Zuani the Red, through two of his sons. According to our origins we should be barbarians, as my host in his palace in Catania once strove to convince me; he was the head of the Sicilian branch, called the panther, because to our old blazon—a shield held aloft by chained unicorns, azure, a swan argent, volant, its throat pierced by a purple arrow—it added a black panther, on a gold field with a fur border, in honor of an illustrious addition to the family. We are quite possibly Norse, as all until the last two, he and me, preserved red hair and blue eyes as the lasting markers of our line, but the only certain point is that I come from sailors, and it is my only vanity; because if we could choose our ancestors, as was normal in great houses, I would have wanted a sailor before anything else; I would like to claim descent from Thamuz, whom, out of the desolation of an evening on the waves, a mysterious voice ordered to witness the death of the Great Pan. Beyond that, I can't boast of anything, not even the blood spilled under the standard of Eteria, those from Crete who passed through Fanar into Russia and Romanian lands.

Even if I cannot be proud of my line, it should be proud of me. It could not have found a better end. Its traits of impetuosity and vigor, a spirit of sacrifice, a natural urge toward greatness, and a certain charm useful for installing ourselves and rising wherever borne by fate, all harmonize in my character, thanks, I believe, to the fact that my veins do not hold opposing bloodlines: my parents were close relations, first cousins. About the same age and both orphans, they were raised together and their attraction flowered early, and in spite of prejudice, it was hallowed in marriage.

I was an only child. I was the reflection of their bright love, they watched warmly as their twin, melded souls were mirrored in my being, they showered me with a thousand attentions. Not even the milk I suckled was foreign. Blessed be the heaven that permitted me a happy childhood. Whenever I think of it, I hear a fluttering, the white flight of doves in the serene sky of a spring morning. It is my earliest memory. It is also a symbol.

But the child so doted was not happy; my soul was always snared by that gentle melancholy felt by too-sensitive beings, so sensitive that even caresses make them suffer, for whom even pleasure is a wound. Long before reading Lucretius I had realized that something bitter echoed in the waters of voluptuousness, the same overwhelming quality contained in the scent of flowers.

I can't imagine many people's life and aging have changed them as little as mine have me. I will be the same until death: an unrepentant dreamer, ever drawn to the distant and mysterious. I was very young when, dropping my toy, I ran into the courtyard to listen to a woman singing on the other side of the alley; in a lisping, weak voice, she mimicked a song that I can almost hear now: "a bird in a tree, a river of pleasure, I sing of a pain beyond any measure . . ." and then she coughed, and breathed a long sigh. After a short while, no one heard the song any longer . . . In the evening, I liked to sit on the porch with Osman, our dog, and watch the stars come up.

The memories of the first years of my life, now that I have returned to the places where I experienced them, and perhaps as a sign of old age, have become more and more vivid, sometimes actual hallucinations. Once in Cişmegiu, I had a vision of myself as a child, as I was a half century ago when under those same trees, my Mamma Sia walked with me, hand-in-hand.

Alongside my parents, Mamma Sia has a place in my heart, our good Mamma Sia, the faithful woman who had been their nanny and now was mine. She was family, some even whispered that she received no salary; she sat at table with us and called us by first names, she would carp and squabble with everyone in the house, where she was in fact the master; my mother didn't and couldn't do a thing.

My mother was a doll, the dearest doll, the sweetest. Her beauty was the talk of the town; if you had seen her unbraiding her hair, thick as burnt honey, or had ever met the deep gaze of her blue eyes beneath black eyebrows, you would have said a white Magdalene, painted in the Italian school during the most languorous days of its decline, had stepped out of its frame. Even though I loved her to the point of idolatry, I felt I did not love her enough, and this thought still fills me with remorse. A song that ends, a flower that wilts, a star that falls, these unfailingly bring her to my mind, and then her icon adopts the dark charm of those lost before their time, and I feel such tenderness that I cannot regard her image except through tears.

With my father, things were different; my feelings for him took shape slowly, as the result of judgment, founded on admiration. A well-kempt tyro with a woman's hands, whose manner and appearance seemed English to Parisians, he embodied rare virtues, true character. His schooling, and the protection of reigning Prince Alexandru-Ioan, with whom he enjoyed great influence, had him named directly to the Court of Appeals and quickly raised to the Supreme Court. He was later a Member of Parliament. The secularization of monastery holdings and our peasant land reform are both due in large part to him. He was the youngest if not the most famous of those well-known men who, after the prince's overthrow, retired permanently from public life. I was in the dawn of youth when, one afternoon, two unfamiliar boyars came to our house and sat with my father behind the doors of the sitting room for more than an hour. Before they left, my father let them alone for a moment and went into the yatak where my mother slept, then came back to walk the unexpected guests out as far as the lane, to their carriage. That evening I learned that Father had asked Mother's blessing to refuse a ministry.

For fear that the tranquility that dominated our nest should be at all disturbed, my father took no decision without asking my mother—a practice which, of course, had its own problems. Because of her, we lived, although amply, somewhat below our means; our life was not as lordly as one might think, and any alteration petrified my mother. The dear woman would never have acquiesced to move from Bucharest; even a visit to the countryside, to take in the vineyards or the baths—may heaven forbid; and those trips in caravan to Borsec or Zaizon must have had a particular atmosphere. Even getting her out of the house was an ordeal. Who would have thought this woman would give birth to a man who would circumnavigate the earth, more than once!

Poor mother, so many problems! She was prone to chill, she was tortured by heat, she could not abide the sun or wind; light made her ill, dark oppressed her, the softest noise made her start in fright. At the sight of blood, she fainted. Parties—and she was often being celebrated—were a chore. She did not try to have real friends; instead, every day a chattering synod would assemble at her home: gossipy droppers-by from the edge of town, reeking of poverty; priests' wives, old babas, fruit-preservers, plain women who read your cards or coffee grounds. Her idea of fun was to dress like a peasant, in a floral skirt and embroidered headscarf, with a necklace made of coral or coins, and to insist she liked folk music better than Italian opera. "Anicuţa has bad taste in people," Aunt Smaranda would say about my mother. And when that woman died and left us large houses with chapels, like at Cişmeaua-roşie, Mother was the one who refused to move there, saying that Podul-de-pământ, or as they used to call it, the Pastrami Shop, was prettier. Maybe she was right: on the lot between St. Constantin and St. Elefterie, from Giafer to Pricopoaia, where today untended chaos reigns, there was a proper garden, nothing but lilacs, fruit trees, grapevines over arched trellises. Chamomile and mallow flooded the courtyard, oleanders were everywhere, plums and lemons, the windows were thick with gardenias, muscatel, fuchsia, pelargonium, wallflowers. And beyond, over the creek, blocking the view, thickly washed with green plants, was the hill of Cotroceni!

My friend stopped here, and smiling, methodically lit a cigarette, ordered coffee, wine. And after a moment, he returned to the thread of his story.

. . . In a brightly lit salon, elegant cucoanas decked with bijouterie and hooped malakoffs, boyars with thick sideburns or imperial mustaches, the order of Nizan glittering at their necks, bow deeply to kiss the hand of an old woman dressed in green, a tiny, desiccated old woman, her hair dyed carrot-orange, her eyes a faded blue. She still has a grand air: she stands straight, her head held high in a spirited gaze, she speaks with precision and vigor. In the seven years since she returned from her last trip to Baden-bis, she has not left the house, and because she sleeps only little and dislikes being alone, after each evening's meal, taken at a setting of twelve pieces, she entertains until late at night.

With her perished one of the last vestiges of the world of yesteryear; she had known a grand age. When she died in 1871, she was approaching eighty-eight years on earth, seventy-two of which she spent a widow, after a short marriage to a Greek beg, a ravenous man-child who stuffed himself on bilberries and succumbed to an intestinal torsion. Afterwards, she decided not to marry again and led a good part of that long life "within," among the most brilliant nobility. Firm in her prejudices to the point of zealotry, anyone would forgive her self-importance as soon as he heard her speak; her gift in this aspect was more amazing than the strength of her mind; to articulate any detail, any bagatelle, she used her own particular expression; when she told an anecdote, it was like she was reading from a fine work of literature. Likewise, she was a pillar of good sense, an edifice; no superstitions for her, no quirks; and she was not to blame for her one oddity, that she dressed only in green and wore no other precious stone than emeralds. Over time, the greens became darker, she hid behind a veil of black lace, and only to lay her in her coffin did they dress her, according to her wish, in the tangerine wool dress she had worn as a bride.

May she rest in peace! I made my gratitude for her into a rule for living; along with her significant fortune, she left me that holy treasure that is tradition, my entire inner being is her creation, only hers; teaching me grand ideals, she awakened in me old aspirations. From her I learned that I have the God-given duty of leadership, I am one of those who through wealth and fame rise above ordinary mortals. Later in life, I was able to face moments of catastrophe solely through the aid of her memory; in the chill of self-doubt and maltreatment, the image of Her Highness always appeared before me, tranquil, dressed in green, with green stones sparkling from head to foot.

I was left with the dear woman every afternoon. I was present while she dressed, an elaborate toilette that continued long into the evening. During this time, she narrated. She had known personally the highest nobility of three-quarters of a century. She had often visited Napoleon I, who once spoke to her, she had been with her father during the Congress of Vienna, she had danced with Emperor Alexander and with Metternich, and in Italy she had received homages from both Chateaubriand and Byron. So as not to lose her father's pension of a Governor's Major-General, which Emperor Nicholas had given her for life, after 1830 she never set foot in France, which, ever since the illicitous war, as she called it, in Crimea, she hated to death. Yet the language she preferred, after Greek of course, was French, an old Court French, wide-ranging and deadly, scented with bergamot and musk. But when she spoke about our family's past, she switched to Romanian, and then the story took on a mystical light; the woman found sublime pairs of words for the long resistance against the pagan hordes, the unexpected martyrdom, the triumph of faith over the bitter road. In a whisper she spoke of the betrayal of two high officials and their cruel sufferings; of the heads, eight in number, that the yatagan severed in less than one hundred years, of flight into Russia, of provoking two wars and inciting Filiki Eteria. Nothing enchanted me as much as these stories; the enthusiasm with which I listened reached its peak when she came to florid memories of her distant childhood, spent entirely in splendor and comfort. The old woman I saw in the mirror, obsessively applying her makeup among candles in daytime, had been one of three esteemed women for whom many hearts had bled. And I regarded, dreamily, the painting in which they appeared, arms around each other's waists, young, flaxen-haired, with blue eyes and black eyebrows, all three: Balasa, Safira, and Smaranda. With these baptisms, their mother, wife of Kaimakam Păuna, bequeathed to each the precious stone chosen by her godmother, binding them by an oath that they would not dress, for their entire lives, in any other color than that of the stone. It sounds like a fairy tale, doesn't it? I promise this is but one detail from the wonderful fairy tale of this princess of gentleness that was my grandmother. One day, I'll tell you the entire story, and you'll learn then, perhaps with surprise, about all her subtle tastes and tiny vanities, her love of flowers and scents, of dear things, adornments and jewels, her appetite for reckless spending that came to us from the Romanian side through her, and not as you might think, from the Greek. Our beauty also came from her. I was curious to know more about my inheritance of unusual inclinations, so I researched my ancestors' personalities, but as witnesses were rare, aside from what I was able to pick up from my old aunt, I did not discover much, and I was unable to find any trace of my strangest tick: I mean my invincible weakness for the Gypsies—you must have noticed how their bitter fate moves me, how I love to sit and listen to them in their scorned language? I learned it as a child, from Stan, an almost blind old man who made pig stew and stayed with us after emancipation, until he died in our courtyard, where he had been born. He had lost his sight and sleep at the same time, and winter or summer, day or night, he sat at the hearth with a pipe in his mouth. He was very fond of me; when I had a fever—I was so easily hexed, the people in my house feared me—I remember how he would take me in his arms and rock me, his eyes in tears. These Gypsy men and women smile at me from the past, with especially friendly faces and white teeth; I first tasted love with a Gypsy girl, a girl of the streets. She wore a red flower on her ear and danced when she walked. I was sixteen. It was cypress season, at night, after a rain. I gave her a galben and forgot to ask her name. And I never saw her again.

In this manner, on various themes, he told one story after another. They showed that no greater care could have been spent on his upbringing and that he had studied seriously under the enlightened oversight of his father, who had planned to send him to some lofty school in Paris, but Cucoana Anicuța, supported by Sia, objected. But neither was he so happily reconciled to the idea of leaving such loving parents, who acted like, and in looks appeared to be, his older brother and sister. He would have lived with them in that withdrawn and comfortable life, until who knows when, if in 1877, just after he turned twenty, war had not broken out. Here I will let him speak again.

I had gone to my father, to announce my decision to leave directly for the army, a decision nothing in the world could alter. The great Alexander Nikolayevich, a Russian Orthodox Caesar, had drawn his sword against the enemy of the nation, and from that moment, alive or dead, I had no honorable place but under the flag of the Holy Empire of the East. With trepidation, my father asked what he should tell my mother—and I will leave you to imagine his stupefaction when I said that the dear woman, to whom I had gone first, had given her permission. What had changed within her remains an enigma. Yet the miracle—I cannot call it anything else— did not end there. Suddenly a grand cucoana emerged out of the little doll. She unlocked the house at Cişmeaua-roşie and turned it into a hospital for the wounded, simply doing what she thought was right, and with such competence that it seemed she had never done anything else. For his part, Father received a commission alongside Prince Gorchakov, whose family was bound to ours by friendship. I also wore one, higher than is given in the heat of battle—I have already told you something of Sergei of Leuchtenberg. If he had lived . . . His death, which I witnessed, was the first in a series of painful trials. When I arrived home again, I found my mother was no more. Like all her family, she did not know how to take care of herself. Suffering a terrible cold during the war's awful winter, she refused to rest and, in accordance with her pride, she stayed on her feet until her illness overcame her. Far from her husband and son, she surrendered her soul in the arms of Mamma Sia, without a complaint, without a tear, calm to the end. The brave soldiers whose wounds she tended wept as they bore her on their shoulders to her grave. The terrors of war had prepared me to survive this blow that, in contrast, destroyed my father; I suffered less from her death than from seeing him survive her. The poor man became unrecognizably feeble and hunched over, with tangled gray hair and a beard, his nails uncut and dark, filthy . . . A rending hopelessness reflected in his glassy eyes, which betrayed, even when he didn't speak, the loss of his mind. His pain at home did not make him forget the bitterness he endured over the loss of Bessarabia; because I didn't learn of his intention in time, he was able to send back the Order of St. Anna, the fifth of six with which our house was honored. I understood immediately that I could do nothing but resign myself: the man had been damned by God. He did not feed himself or sleep, he drank constantly and smoked without stopping. He persisted in this way a few months more, then went to take his eternal place alongside

Mother. Soon after, I laid Mamma Sia at their feet and I was alone in the world.

I needed some time to recover. I hardly left the house, I began to take late walks far outside the city. In the course of these walks, I noticed that when I crossed the Marmizon Bridge, I always saw one unusually beautiful girl. I shortly became apprehensive of missing her, and I was sad when I did. Without my noticing, the hap of seeing her developed into a need, and more and more emotions accumulated; day or night, her face arose before my mind, I could not think of the young woman without becoming disturbed, and when I encountered her I was overwhelmed with a timidity I had not known before, one which prevented me from talking to her for some while. What seemed strange to me in this story was not that I had fallen for someone—my turn had simply come—but that I had fallen for her in particular, since, by my nature, I was usually attracted to women with dark skin, as dark as possible, and she was flaxen-haired and pale, almost pallid, so do not be surprised, my friend, if I tell you that although I loved her with passion, her corporality, even from close, did not awaken in me the first thought of desire; what ignited my mysterious feeling of love was only pity. When I saw Wanda, that was her name, weep as she described her life, her pains at the hands of her stepmother, her father who was Polish and, she gave to understand, a drunk, how she suffered taking constant care of his brood, patching clothes and cleaning stains, and then when I learned they were planning to traffic her, as they had her older sister, I decided, in order to save her, I would leave prejudice aside and lift her to my level. I knew only too well what gossip would follow my actions; the judgments of the living did not concern me, but the dead demanded my explanation, they returned during frigid nights of insomnia, standing in rows like in old Greek icons, against a red-gold background and rigid in their auric kaftans, those proud archontes carrying their decapitated heads, turning their disgusted, unyielding gazes away from me, the traitor. I did not have the strength to resist, and I let myself be cast about by the will of fate. My year of mourning was ending, only a little more remained before the day we would be engaged, I had even ordered the rings.

Then, on the morning I was bringing them, engraved with our names, back from the jeweler, who did I find waiting on the bench by the door—I was still living at Podul-de-pământ, or Calea Plevnei, as the name became—but Cucoana Elenca, wife of the Exchequer, one of the most imposing of Mother's neighborhood friends; she had something to tell me. I had a premonition . . . I invited her in. She wept briefly for Cucoana Anicuţa, but as soon as her tears had gone, she vehemently denounced my plans, saying that even were Wanda an honest girl I would be committing a great sin, but in no case could I proceed with some tartlet who slept with the dregs of society and had already had call for the doctor and the midwife. I was petrified.

"If you don't believe me, my boy," she added, "keep watch one night after eleven, see for yourself how she lets her amoretto in through the window. I can even tell you who it is: Fane, the widow's boy, the painter, the one who plays the harmonium."

A stake went through my heart, my ears started to hum and the house spun around me. It was a mortal blow. However calamitous my circumstances seemed, I did not lose my senses, I judged things coolly. The fact that she had made mistakes—before I met her, lacking as she did any attention or upbringing, surrounded by bad examples and bad advice—wounded but did not surprise me; yet to mock me in this way, and with this kind of man, on the eve of our engagement, that exceeded any measure and I could never forgive her. And I recalled the time I asked my mother to tell my future, and she explained that I would have part of all the happiness life affords, except love. I thanked Cucoana Elenca and told her to rest easy. When Wanda arrived for dinner as usual, she found me dressed for travel, tightening the straps on my suitcase. I lied, I said I had to visit the countryside for a few days, unexpectedly. Throughout the meal, I scrutinized her, stealthfully; aside from gentleness and guilelessness, I could read nothing in her face or in her eyes. Then the pain of doubt bored into my chest, especially since it seemed utterly unbelievable that this creature would scorn the most enviable luck imaginable for one of her station. We both left in the hansom; her I left at her house, while I followed the road to Cotroceni, made a wide circle around the city, and returned via Capu-podului around evening to Cişmeaua-roşie. I entered our long abandoned chapel, where I had not set foot since childhood, I lit a torch-stub forgotten from another time and, begging the intercession of the spirit of both Princess Smaranda and the One Above, I sank into prayer.

The heavenly Spirit did not hesitate to pour over me; in its light I understood that everything was working toward my salvation, which could come only through Wanda's betrayal or her hasty destruction. God would not permit our scutcheon, which since 1812 had shown the crown on the breast of the eagle with two Russian heads, to be jeopardized. I whispered, "Not ours, Lord, but to your eternal name be honor and praise!" I was terrified to realize what horror I had intended to commit! . . . I left that place resigned to my fate, and restored. The fearsome thoughts that had churned within me gave place to trepidation and the wish that the Exchequer's wife had not lied; and when, two hours later, I had living proof of my betrayal, within my very pain I found relief. Now that I had lost her who had embodied my dream of love, I told myself there was nothing left but to forget her.

That act lay beyond my powers. Not even today, after thirty years, has my love for her ceased to burn; in fact, time and distance have transformed it into something mystical: I don't love Wanda herself anymore, not the one who, if she is still on earth, is changed, wilted, and aged; I love her unspeakably tender and sweet memory. And in the women who have taken their turns through my life since then, I have loved only that which resembled her: in some her yellow hair or hazel eyes, in others the sadness of her smile, the undulation of her gait, or the melody of her voice that charmed me so . . . Now you see why I once agreed with Paşadia, when he said that he saw nothing in love but fetishism. Yes, fetishism, fetishism . . .

He shrugged and flicked away the cigarette which, as he spoke, had turned silently and completely to ash. He ordered fruit, a stronger wine, another round of coffee. And eating, and sipping, he continued.

To lose my senses, I threw myself into the whirlpool of party life so enthusiastically that my unbridled dissipation caused Bucharest society alarm. For a year, at Cişmeaua-roşie, where I had moved, I threw one party after another, from night until the white of dawn. I gathered a large court of the most rotten of people: when I went hunting or toured the monasteries, I brought a retinue of at least twenty overstuffed carriages, not only the domestics and provisions but also my band of musicians. We never lacked for anything, however insignificant; this host of people excelled at meeting my wishes and pleasing me; often their zeal went too far: if one day I mentioned I found a certain woman attractive, that night I would find her in my sheets. Some men brought me their wives, and brothers their sisters. But I couldn't keep up with so much spending; after I burned through the cash I had inherited, I took on debt after debt. Once I reached rock bottom, Nenea Scarlat, known as "the ibrik," an awful, ancient boyar, a pander, a trader of horses and other things, lent to me at savage rates of interest. I tangled myself up worse and worse; my tenants paid their leases and rents with my own notes of debt, which naturally I had to accept. Then I would sign others, and I signed constantly, sometimes without even seeing what, until the morning I sent to Nenea Scarlat for some notes and he responded that he was weaning me off the teat, and soon I'd have to clear out all my accounts. And he encouraged me, grinning, to sell what I had of my own will rather than make him put it on the block; he would always find a buyer. I entreated him to find me a few more coins, and without delay; it was the night before my birthday and I wanted, for a particular reason, to celebrate properly. I gave him a few of Princess Smaranda's settings, some brooches, to pawn.

"We've had some luck," he said, coming back with good money, "a lot of luck. If I had arrived a quarter hour later, you would have been left empty-handed. My friend was on his way out of Bucharest."

I didn't ask who the mysterious money-bawd was; did it matter? I charged Nenea Scarlat with the preparations and invitations for the next day, and I locked myself until evening in the salon dedicated to "the Inestimable" and burned my family's papers. I ate at Hugues, alone, and then I wandered at random through the streets. I will never forget that foggy and cold night in April, the full moon like a custard scented with plum blossoms, the night that was to be my last. Don't think I wanted to end my days because I no longer had my inheritance; just the opposite: I had frittered everything I had away because I had already decided I had had enough of this life and would end it; its tableau intensified my inborn sadness, its pleasures gave me only deception and disgust. And for the occasion of my disappearance from among the living, I had chosen the day on which I turned twenty-three. I planned to step out during the party and not come back; no one would discover what had become of me, the mystery of my death would remain forever unsolved—I had taken every measure. Before dawn, the gentle ghosts of my childhood rose up before me, to pity but not to dissuade me; the serenity with which those of my blood welcome death did not abandon me. When I returned calmly home, I found a slip of paper, delivered late that evening, which ordered me to appear without fail in court the next morning. Earlier that day, my uncle Iorgu had been killed.

Even though I was the child of first cousins, I never met or even saw him. The mismatched marriage that had produced him, and misunderstandings that came later, had alienated him and his father from the rest of the family. To his natural enmity for them, a feeling envenomed by the impossibility of causing them harm, they had responded with a deep scorn which today I do not wish to share. He was a man! Not content to laze around on the production of his inheritance, he busied himself with challenging work; he leased acreages, fishing ponds, customs houses, salt mines, post offices, he acquired broad interests in lumber and wool, he built an inn in Bucharest and a lock on the Danube, and fortune richly repaid his daring and industry. The war, during which he was the army's great quartermaster, had made him the richest man in the country, although he still spent sums on trivial pleasures, one galben or two, with a money-bawd for emergencies. In the struggle for his inheritance, he didn't hesitate to use his strongest methods. Recently, he had won, through arguments and bribes, his old suit against those unsuitable inheritors of Toroipanu on the Neajlov, and set out to complete a survey of the land. At the place where the road entered the neighboring forest, he suddenly found himself halted and surrounded by a number of armed peasants. He stood and drew his two pistols, but before he could fire, he was bound to the steps of his carriage and murdered in a fury.

I was invited to attend the breaking of the seals, placed the evening before across his sordid dwelling on Mântuleasa Street. I would have never imagined that anyone, however miserly, could live in such squalor. I did not involve myself in the audit of his assets, aside from a moment of vivid amazement when they opened his colossal iron strongbox. It wasn't the treasures there that surprised me, but the brooches I spied, the brooches I had given to Nenea Scarlat to pawn. Then all of my notes of debt were discovered; a thick packet. What else can I say? They pawed and pecked through everything, they nitpicked every scrap of paper, but they found no trace of his will, which meant that at the very hour I had set for my own end, I found myself, as the victim's closest relative, master of his enormous fortune.

At first this twist of fate, as unexpected as it was happy, pleased those who had been living off my largesse, the leeches. They thought the days of bounty had returned. Their disappointment and resentment, however, arrived quickly. It might be said that I inherited not only my unknown uncle's estate but also some of his quirks. I soon closed up the house on Cişmeaua-roşie and moved to Mântuleasa; the horses, coaches, pure-bred dogs, I let everything go, I released the extra domestics, I drove off my friends, and I laid a cross on the parties. And I have not wasted another day here, beyond what was needed to arrange my affairs, in the prospect of a permanent absence.

I have not completely revised my intention to vanish, I have only changed the manner, choosing distance instead of death. If I would remove myself in any case, what is there here that still could tempt me? Power, perhaps? But in the country where my father declined to become a minister and my great-grandfather to become a lord, what could I desire? And furthermore, I would not sacrifice my liberty to wear the star of the Empire on my sash. Starting now, my only masters will be imagination and caprice. Doing otherwise would prove me unworthy of so much fortune.

And I have had it by the cartload. Let me explain. I was only going to stay one more night in Bucharest. Before going to bed, I went to take my passport from a chest of drawers, but the drawer was too full; when I pulled, it stuck. It took me an hour to yank and wiggle the drawer until it bested me with another feat of chance: the damned passport, which had been on top, fell behind the drawer, and the drawers could not be removed completely. I wanted to take an axe to the chest, but in my weakness for antiques—it was an Empire piece, in an utterly ugly mahogany—I spared it, satisfying myself with wedging a back panel free. Inside, I found my passport and more: a large, crumpled yellow envelope with five seals in black wax. On it was written, "My Testamente," with an inflected "e."

Shaken from head to toe by such a chill as I had never experienced, I looked quickly around, even though I knew I was alone in the house. Outside the blinds, October rain rapped against the glass. I opened the envelope and, holding my breath, I read the last wishes of my uncle: he left his entire estate, all property real and personal, to Eforiei Hospital. With awful horror, I stared at the weapon which, had it fallen into other hands than mine, would have killed me, and I continued to watch it until a few moments later, when it turned to ash. It is possible what I did was not right, but I will only answer to the Eternal, who, as my Aunt Smaranda would say, measures our sins by a scale of his own, and often makes mistakes. And I don't blush at the fact that a few lines of writing made me quiver, as many times as I have steadfastly stared Death in the face; no, because this was my inheritance, and nothing else in the world is holy to me, this was everything, more than honesty, health, life, and if it had been necessary, in that night, the memory of which still disturbs me, to do something more serious than obliterate a scrap of paper, well, believe me when I tell you, I would not have hesitated . . . I was not poor in spirit!

It would have been a shame to let that wealth fall through my fingers; without it, my family line, just before its twilight, would never have returned to its true, its only natural fate, a free life on the waves. I am convinced that the noble use I gave this wealth has redeemed it, more than my uncle's decision would have, from the crimes with which he procured it. In thirty years of maritime peregrination, I have been afloat longer, perhaps, than all my sailor ancestors combined, and often I felt them rejoicing within me, as I bore their standard forth, a swan pierced by an arrow, over seas those dear people never imagined, over every sea . . .

He motioned for the bill to the waiter circling us. The establishment had emptied. We left as well. Outside, the sky was clear and the air was cold.

"Yes, amice," he said, after a few steps, "the inheritance! If not for that, I would never have returned. The 1907 émeute gave me pause for thought, and so, to relieve my heart of the continual fear of losing my estate, I decided, finally, this year, this spring, to return and to sell it, to sell even at a loss. I've received ridiculous offers, and from whom do you imagine? Peasants! It must be written in the stars that I would make these people rich; no, sincerely, you don't know how brazen they are, and on my word, how different they are from those I knew in my childhood at Cişmeaua Roşie, who hung around like dogs at the foot of the stairs, in front of Aunt Smaranda, almost blinded by her greatness; and today their children are the new leaders, fixing their gazes on me and speaking man to man. And I wonder where their community acquired so much cash that they can buy up thirty-eight thousand pogoane of land like it was nothing. I had imagined that the buildings in Bucharest would go just as easily, and I was pitifully mistaken; the most run-down property, a poor hovel on Bărăţie, has been the topic of eight months of conversation between me and some desperate merchant-types; not even when I sold my petroleum stocks in Amsterdam—petroleum that brought me over seventy-five percent profit—was there such haggling. They can sense I'm in a hurry.

"Even with the charm of these dear memories, my stay in this city has seemed, from the hour I arrived, a state of exile, as any place is, wherever I am on dry land; only my love of flowers brings me peace, the only passion my longing for the sea could not overcome. Like my great-grandmother Păuna, who was the first to bring several varieties into Wallachia and sowed them over many pogoane at Pajera, I am wild about flowers; for my orchids, not for me—I am only their guest—I purchased the manueline quinta which, on the shore of the ocean, in a paradisiacal Lusitanian corner, once gave refuge to a royal love. In the balsam humidity of its great evenings, with apiaries and quick waters, I dream, between two departures;

in the lap of its hanging gardens, as soon as I feel my end is coming, I will embark on my final voyage . . .

. . . "But why is everything closed, is it really that late?" And looking at the glittering November sky: yes, it was very late; the hunter with golden weapons, Orion, was setting, fearful of the Scorpion that scuttled across the threshold of the East. Dawn, however, was still a ways off, it was time to go to my place to drink.

I departed Str. Modei when they lit the streetlamps, still dizzy from what I had heard.

Desiring to prevent, as much as possible, anyone recognizing him in Bucharest, where he wanted to be alone with his memories and unobstructed in his circulation, *** attempted, before returning, to change his appearance. He let his hair grow, including his mustache and beard, and adopted a simple and quiet manner; he succeeded so well that, after almost a year, catching sight of himself in the mirror, he would wonder whether it was really he. Another person had taken over his being and soon had a name as well: people in the places he visited called him "Conu Pantazi," which gave him reason to suppose that his new avatar had been mistaken for a doppelgänger by that name, and he wondered how it was they had not met.

He showed me the photograph of his true face, clean-shaven, hair trimmed, with short sideburns—a compleat gentleman in the elegant dress of a ship's captain. I regarded it without emotion, since it did not look like my friend since the world began, another version of myself; rather, this other whom I now encountered, not without some smidgeon of melancholy, was nothing but a temporary guise, shortly to be dismissed, forever.

The fear that this disappointment would diminish the charm of our friendship was just as vain as the hope that I would go home early. For a week I did not go home at all. I moved in with Pantazi—I will continue to call him so—and when the snow fell and a sharp wind blew, he cloistered himself in his tightly wrapped home, where it was dark as night. There was no need to go out; his host had learned all his tastes and bent over backwards to satisfy them. The beds—mine was set up in the salon—were always turned down, the table set, the candelabra lit. The tile stoves rumbled. In the somnolence of our long vigils, his confession, of a life lived as a wise citizen of the universe, unrolled without compulsion, complete. In this, he revealed the only motive for sadness that stoked my envy: the man had been too happy. Nothing more restful than that mode of life, nothing sweeter. Neither one of us thought to change it, although the bad weather had gone, until one morning—we knew morning had come by the chocolate we had been served—the host came in, angry and red, to tell Pantazi that a man was calling, a man who swore horribly and had a dog. He had treated her with an unimaginable rudeness. Pantazi asked me to see who it could be, while he and the French woman drew the curtains and snuffed the candles.

The daylight and a vibrating, snub-nosed dog in a red wrap entered along with Pirgu. We learned that Paşadia, returned to the city, had spent the night going from one establishment to another in search of us, and he had charged this man, if he found any trace, to invite us to dine with him. Pantazi accepted without hesitation. He asked Gore who his company was, as it growled at Pantazi and began to bark.

"It belongs to Haralambescu," he explained. "Tinculina Gaiduri has a dog in heat, also a pug, a big girl, and I'm taking him to her. I've turned into a canine pimp."

This round of evenings with Paşadia was controlled, dignified; Pirgu favored us only occasionally with his presence, in passing, and then he only spoke about politics. "The liberals," he insisted, "were run out of town." By New Year's Day 1911 at the latest, that is, in three weeks, the conservatives would come to power, the boyars. "Take's been wiped out." And Pirgu would adopt a serious air, befitting the high post he said he would receive in the new government.

Even though I knew his immeasurable avarice—he would stick his nose in shit to find a dime—I could tell immediately that he was not after the salary, but another object of desire, and I would not have believed it if he himself, on Christmas Eve, over one little ţuica that turned into two—"the adult dosage"—had not told me.

He had been planning to marry for some time already, for the money, of course, but however often he had tried, he had been shown the door; even when the girl happened to like him, her parents would put their foot down, and this leperhood must, he thought, come from the fact that he had no "career." What else did he lack to make a wife happy; as he insisted, was he not handsome and young, "mannered" and cultured? And in the face of a minister's guarantee that his dear chief of staff is a serious boy with a future, a minister ready to stand up at his wedding, who could object? Once he had his appointment, it had to work, they would see this "heavy," this "boss" with full pockets, with a palace of a house in Bucharest, vineyards in Mieilor Valley, a country estate who knows where, bunches of acres no joke, and a single father-in-law with a single lung. Gore sang, "He's got it all! He's got it all!" I interrupted to ask if he had thought of the two paraphernalia that could follow: kids and horns?

"Don't you worry," he said calmly. His state had taken of both beforehand. "That kind of paraphernalia is easy to deal with, they won't come into play."

I was perplexed. I asked him who would give him the appointment.

"Paşa," he whispered mysteriously, in my ear, even though we were alone.

"You think he can?"

"Oho! You can't even imagine how connected that old goat is. All he has to do is lay them on the table and you'll see how all plays out."

"And why wouldn't he?" I wanted to draw him out. By way of an answer, Gorică whistled two short notes, wagging two fingers beside his head. Then he took his leave, walking backward. And at the door he made the sign of Harpocrates.

During one of those nights between Christmas and New Year's, I was on Calea Victoriei, where reigned an unusual energy. Newspaper vendors were ripping open their packs, crying as loud as their mouths could manage, "The government falls!" In front of the palace gardens, someone called to me from a closed carriage. It was Pirgu.

"Good doctor," he said, "could you go by Paşadia's and tell him to drop everything and go, right away, this very evening, as fast as he can, to take care of my affairs, to pull his strings? But I mean right away."

I asked why he would not go himself.

"I just don't have the time," he explained, "I'm busy with the burial: Mişu died; I need to give his inconsolable widow a helping hand; tough times show you who your friends are. I'm on my way now from the Jewish cemetery to the newspaper. Ah! Such a fracas over the houses, it turns out Faibish, the elder Nachmansohn, was dead broke, they built the houses on a lot under the name of the late balabusta, Mişu's mother; she dropped her whole fortune. Eh, and now she's wiped out: Mişu left them to little Rachel, as he should—you think she's dumb?—her first husband, Penchas, also left everything to her; you should see her in mourning, the little devil in a dress, yes, yes! Such a minx this woman, mon cher, I mean, really!—Mişu's busy croaking and we're in the next room . . . tu comprends? What a bloodsucker, she wore me out. Just get over there, before the old man leaves, that bastard; I can count on you, right?" And with a curse he ordered the carriage forward. "Come to the funeral tomorrow," he shouted with his head out the side, as it moved away, "I'm giving a speech."

✦

Profundum est cor super omnia—et homo est—
et quis cognoscet eum?
—Jer. 17:9

Armed with the boldness born of asking on another's behalf, I knocked at Paşadia's a quarter hour later. He was at home: toward one end of the courtyard, the lamps of his carriage flickered.

This time, I was not led directly into his study, as usual; the old valet who opened the door, relieved me of my coat and hat, asked me to wait. When I entered, the vestibule was lit only by the flame of a few gnarled sticks burning happily in the wide hearth; their movement strangely animated the canvases on the walls; they gave startling windows onto the past, scenes from a world of martyrs and passion. Leaning on spears, the centurions of Domitian or Decius and the cavalry of wild beasts delectated on the raw agony of crucified virgins and young men pierced with arrows, under the somber rush of clouds over melancholy branches. I was in Paşadia's home. In those frames I found the symbol of his soul's distress. The candelabra was lit and multiplied in the mirrors. After a brief while, the valet returned to say I was invited up.

For the first time, I climbed the staircase that two baroque sphinx guarded, and I was led through several rooms packed, even more so than the first floor, with precious objects; I was conducted through the atmosphere of a museum, not a home. At the last threshold, I stopped a few moments, in surprise.

Doubtless it was not to attend a rendezvous, or to partake of a night of gambling, that Paşadia had donned his tails and his lens, his cross and stars. Yet his dress was nothing in comparison with the alteration in his being I found, as I approached and we began to speak. He seemed more youthful, his movements and his face had lost any trace of weariness, his eyes sparkled, even his voice sounded different, clearer, metallic. I found it hard to accept his assurances that he could not remember having ever been more bored.

An utterly unexpected calamity had befallen the dear man. A high-ranking Austrian personage, on his way to Egypt with his wife, had stopped in Bucharest for three days. Upon arrival, he had searched out Paşadia, whom he knew from school, and now neither he nor she would leave him in peace; he was supposed to accompany her to Furnica's to pick out a few Romanian blouses. And they insisted Paşadia would not miss the banquet that the consul would hold that evening, in their honor.

He hated, in his mind, in his soul, to be obligated to participate in such dull things. At the same time, I wondered—knowing that he would relive for a moment or two the life for which he was meant, his true life—whether he would not feel deeply disturbed by a burgeoning, tardy regret for its abandonment? I observed him surreptitiously. Closed and cold as ever, he was impenetrable, but undeniably, throughout his being, something old and very noble lamented its end.

I said that were I in his place, I would feel flattered, even moved; these people were treating him as kindly as they could, they showed feelings of deep friendship.

"You are mistaken," he replied. "If they do, it is only self-interest. This trip is a cover for an important political mission. The Balkans have been smoldering for three years; the chancelleries are working in haste. And they have been so thoughtful as to remember an old friend . . . No, believe me—gratis, they only do evil. Good or even just for pleasure, never."

Since the conversation had turned to friendship and doing good, I decided it was the proper moment to state what had brought me to him. He smiled.

"I might be as crazy as people say, but make Pirgu respectable, just like that, no!"

I had heard him, however, recently and more than once, solemnly promise his total support to his inseparable Gore, dispelling his fears of failure.

"Not only," he added, "have I not pushed for his appointment, I have taken special care to prevent it, and it is not the first time I have done so; do you think, scoundrel that he is, he would not have found something by now, that he would not have become chief of staff, prefect, general secretary, member of parliament; that he would not have married, and well, if I had not interposed myself? It is certainly the most correct thing I have done in my life, the most honest; any other course of action would have been immoral. And furthermore, if I allowed him to rise, I would lose him; he would abandon me, and it would be very difficult to do without his services.

It's unfortunate. To be able to hunt effortlessly and without soiling my hands in the swamps of vice, I had to make nice with this hyena, I had to feed it, to endure its stench. But what do you enjoy in Pirgu's company? I cannot believe you find any fun in his dumb triviality. I have wanted to warn you for some time; he is more dangerous than you imagine, he is capable of anything, he is not one of those whose own laziness saves him from implication in crime. He has more than one on his conscience. Beware: he is set against you, unable as he yet is to do you something serious, he is content to slobber over you; recently he spent an entire evening ridiculing you with Poponel, yes, that Poponel, the one whose little affairs of manners you leap to defend, with the same naïveté with which you trotted over here for Pirgu.

I have had the displeasure to note your culpable weakness for all that is stigmatized and déclassé, all that is corrupt, ruptured, and wrecked, and I cannot excuse you, even if I supposed you were only researching your 'sketches,' because that would mean you buy your shoddy goods much, much too dearly.

La bohème, odious, unclean, la bohème kills, and often it's more than a figure of speech.

As I care more for you than for your friendship, I am not afraid to upset you, and I have allowed myself this indiscreet sanction, which I extend to include the entire mode of life you have recently adopted. I will withdraw it, however, and be ready to make honorable amends, if you can assure me that you are happy, that after these moments of oblivion you do not hear the howls of your wounded dignity.

You know, he continued, without waiting for my response, you know how precarious, how pitiful my life was for a long while, you'll admit I had every right to call myself a Talmudical mamzer. You know that I wandered for years and years—grande mortalis aevi spatium—through the void, for nothing. Well, now I long for that time of privation and tumult, and lack, and humiliation; I am nostalgic . . . then, I was content. But as soon as the persecution ceased and I suddenly reached the situation I had long ago given up any hope of attaining, my discontent began.

I was far from a Romantic, yet my self-esteem suffered when I saw that those thirty years of austerity and trials, thirty years of sacrifice, study and labor had not achieved what a few nights in the company of the all-powerful wife of a board chairman did. Soon I came to the conviction that my dizzying success was nothing but fate's sadistic demonstration of how far irony could go. All I had so ravenously desired, the power, money, honors, not only did they give me no satisfaction, but they also irritated and discomforted me; the laurels offended, even the pleasure of revenge began to fade. For me the choice was simple: I needed either the energy to hold fast until the finale—and, by fooling myself, to demonstrate that the moral bankruptcy of my life was also a fraud—or the elegance to sound my withdrawal. I possessed such elegance. And as I still had a life to live, albeit one without hope or purpose, I decided that it was pointless to stave off my genius for wrongdoing, which always, since my first youth, has arrived to tempt me in the night.

Those who knew me were surprised I did not expatriate myself. You'll remember the story of the Italian who arrived in Paris, during the reign of Louis XIV, was immediately incarcerated in the Bastille, and forgotten for thirty-five years. In the first days of the Regency, his case was reviewed and his innocence completely proven; when he was told that his liberty would be returned to him, the poor man asked mournfully what he was supposed do with it, and requested they leave him in prison. I was like him, perhaps even his reincarnation. What would I have done, anywhere else? No other place in the world holds any interest for me, and nothing, absolutely nothing brings me pleasure, even those things that were once so dear—learning, art, reading, writing, if I still dabble in these things, it is only to kill time; to put it simply, I can say, without being rhetorical, that I no longer live; for some time, my soul has drowsed in Death's waiting room. The waiting is almost over. Oblivion comes next, deep oblivion . . ."

"Oblivion," I exclaimed, "never! The literary oeuvre you have created over thirty years, once it comes to light, will make you immortal."

"No! It will perish along with me. When I will finally close my eyes, a faithful hand will destroy all the writing in this house. You will have noticed that in my study, the cabinets are built into the walls and covered by curtains. This is to hide the fact that they have no bottom: they open onto a room below. Before the officers come to place their seals on the door, from below, unseen, the hand will do its duty."

I trembled, knowing he was not one to joke. These works were destined to perish unknown, when they would have gained the admiration of the ages, works that could have come from the quill of Cardinal de Retz or the pencil of Saint-Simon, pages worthy of Tacitus. I was overwhelmed by a rending sense of regret.

"Raised abroad from a young age," he began again, "I had no way of knowing that here we are at the gates of the Orient, where the moral scale is completely upside-down, where nothing is taken seriously. With a stubbornness that says nothing for my intelligence, but which I do not regret, and were I to do it over, I would change nothing—I refused to assimilate, to adapt, although I had been taught, 'si Romae vivis, romano vivite more.' Naturally, I was considered an outsider, I made everyone my enemy. Disgusted, I had to engage in a battle for which I was not made. Seeing that it was difficult to destroy me with insults, as my bite was more venomous than theirs, a conspiracy of silence greeted what I began to publish. Realizing that my only means of revenge would be to leave nothing behind that they could use or enjoy, and as I lack subaltern vanities, I welcomed the conspiracy and stuck to myself. 'Ungrateful fatherland, you will not have my bones'—the inscription Scipio Africanus asked for on his tomb. I will leave my bones, but not the fruit of my mind, not my thought!"

He looked at the clock, apparently worried. I rose to leave.

"Sit a while longer," he said, "we will leave together, you will accompany me there." And in a low voice, "It's safer."

I paced again through the succession of salons, where among all the flowers, aside from the natural ones, an age persisted as though embalmed, with its farded Olympus and pastoral sweetness: a gallant age. But in the most decorated of these rooms, in vivid contrast with the delicate wonders found there, a melancholic face rose from one shadowy corner, the face of a completely other type of person than those men or women who smiled, in menace or sweetness, from other frames. I paused. The resemblance to Pașadia was so complete that I would have said it was him, only somewhat younger, dressed in the fashion of a boyar from one hundred years ago.

"It is my great-grandfather," said Pașadia. "Of my entire family, he is the only one for whom I feel any sympathy, so I didn't burn his portrait like the others. He was a Bergami. His pride, in the glow of that prestige which women's eyes award to those who have taken a life, allowed him to pass from the train of Lady Ralu's carriage to her bed. He received, as payment, the estate of Măgura and the knight's scepter. As you see, the chip did not fall far from the block, and I believe the condition of his soul must have been much like my own, because he, in the flower of his age and with his full knowledge, allowed himself to be poisoned.

"This portrait is one of the few things here that belong to me. The rest is rented."

We descended the stairs slowly, continuing to speak. Below, two valets awaited us alongside Iancu Mitan, the major-domo. Behind the doors, other domestics watched us curiously. The trap started quickly, and soon we had reached Str. Vienna.

"If you meet Pirgu," he said as we parted, "tell him I have done as I thought best, and that I am leaving tonight . . . for the mountains."

Rakes' Twilight

Vous pénétrerez dans les familles, nous peindrons
des intérieurs domestiques, nous ferons du drame
bourgeois de grandes et de petites bretêches.

—Montselet

Toward spring, these departures became more and more frequent, and for longer spells. Upon his return, Paşadia would invite us to dine with him. Presupposing he might need to discuss something with Pantazi, with whom, each day that passed, he was more tightly bound by questions that implicated only the two of them, I developed the habit of leaving them alone, once we had our coffee, for an hour or two, as did Pirgu.

I would leave together with this man, but not without taking care to learn, before we reached the gate, which way he wanted to go, so that I could depart in the opposite direction. He asked me once where I was going. I said to the Academy.

"I didn't know," he said, "it was open again; I'm surprised no one told me. They'll mess it up, you'll see. Billiards is out of fashion; no one plays a little massé or a little three-cushion except guys who sell peanuts on the street, and it's too bad: those were fun games."

He wanted to tag along. I explained that I was going not to the billiard Academy, but the Romanian Academy. He asked what I was doing there and was sincerely disappointed to hear I was going to read. He admonished me.

"Nene, when are you going to give this stuff up? When? You'll turn your brains to mush with all this bookwork. Do you want to end up like Paşadia? Did you ever ask yourself what it matters if you know who cut the cord for Mohammed, or who pulled the cross out first at the feast of the Baptism? Nothing. You're going to rot your brains. Real science is something else, the science of life, and you don't know squat about it. You won't learn that in books.

"They were talking about you today, before you came, they said you were working on a novel of manners, set in Bucharest, and I could barely keep from laughing. I mean, really: you and Bucharest manners. Maybe Chinese manners, as far as that goes, because you might as well be Chinese. How are you supposed to know manners, when you don't know anybody? Do you ever go anywhere, ever see anyone? Aside from us, I mean, maybe if you wrote about Paşa, me, Panta—with anyone else you won't know what you're doing . . . ah, yes, maybe my friend Poponel. Now, if you visited some homes, met some families, that would change things, you'd see how much you'd have to write about, what characters! I know a place . . ."

I beat him to it:

"To the Arnoteanus, the true Arnoteanus."

He waved off any doubts. Then, in confidence:

"There's spreath and spoils, it's a big game that goes on 'til morning, we bring the meretrixies, goes without saying; the guys got the purse, we're on the side, two Holy Unmercenaries."

As I offered unto him, for the umpteenth time, the oath with which I had saved myself from his boring insistence, for the last six months, that we enter that cursed house, I would never have believed that very soon, on the occasion of another meal with Paşadia, he would find his desire sated. If I ultimately had one regret, it was only that I had not helped him achieve his end a little quicker.

A bit fed up with the highfalutin scholars, I felt a desire to play, to laugh. The way Gorică once made me laugh, from the middle of the day until late in the evening, had ransomed, as far as I was concerned, all his sins. It was as though he had gone mad; there were moments when Paşadia nearly booted him out. I had never seen such rabid glee in him, broad and buffo as all hell, an odd glee and yet unforced, and whose motive he explained only toward the end, and in passing: his father had died.

The condolences which Pantazi and I hurried to present him, he cut short; Gorică begged us to be serious.

"I'd understand," he conceded, "if you felt bad that God didn't save me from this pest before now."

Eh, if Sumbasacu Pirgu had croaked ten to twelve years before, if he had let those eight children (of the seventeen they began with) each have their twenty thousand lei, did we think Gore would have ended up what he was: an au pair for the dissolute? What a man he would have become! The most brilliant lawyer ever known, glory of the Romanian bar. He would have defended Paşadia against accusations of sexual assault, and he would have gotten him off, by proving he was impotent. Lawyer and university professor. He would have dabbled in literature in his lost hours, would have mocked morals, would have scribbled plays—bad ones, of course, histories—and with long dialogues strung together between characters from different periods, would have played the leading roles himself, stuttering, snorting, raging. And would these have been the extent of his literary activities? No! Spokesman for the most holy democratic demands, he would have argued in the *National Advisor* for distribution of estates among the peasants and for universal suffrage. And with the force of a single speech, no emptier or drier than those putrescences exspurgated under the roof of the Mitropolia, he would arrive. As distinguished as he was, he would become a diplomat; for this he would need curiosities like Poponel, and at the end of the day, why not: didn't he have Paşadia handy? But his fondest dream would be to live on the land, like a patriarch; he would have pushed a plow, pruned his vines . . .

"It is a marvel," I said to him, "but now that you find yourself a happy heir, what do you want to do?"

"I want to be a whorehouse regular," he responded, "all over Crucea-de-piatră, to have my own bit of ass and my own fling-stinks and my own poontang, and I want to get myself named cantor in a church; and then, when I'm old, I want to become a monk, on my honor! And they'll see, God's servant, Brother Gherasim, or Gideon, or Gerontie, cantor at Darvari Hermitage near Icoană, surprised to hear when it's his turn to read: 'contra' or 'pass.'" And to give us proof of his vocation, he sang through his nose like a priest for almost three quarters of an hour, in a depraved mixture of hymns and popular songs: "Sweet Springtime" and "From Cherry to Cherry," "Christ Is Risen" and "Ma parole d'honneur mon cher," "Let Us Praise the Lord" and "I-ha-ram-bam-ba." Pantazi laughed until he cried, Pașadia weathered the storm. But soon Gore fell quiet, widened his eyes in fright, raised his right index finger to his ear, and sat stone still. Pantazi asked what it was.

"What, don't you hear?" he said, "The trumpet sounds, the tricolor rises!" And he hollered desperately, "Give, give my gun to me, I'll die on the field of victory, not like a slave in slavery, give, give me my horse!" He clambered onto his chair and tried to scooch it forward, but it snagged on the rug; he fell against an icebox, he popped back up unharmed, so spry and light-footed he barely touched the ground; he showed us how he would dance across the Carpathians, from the Tisa to the Nistru, dance the great hora, the hora of the union of all Romanians, and he groaned and chirped: "You wit flowahs in your cap, you wit flowahs in your cap, just like that, just like that, hey hup hey hup!" Then he stepped out of the room for a moment; when he came back, his pant-legs pulled up to his knees and his shirttails out, he looked drunk and very sad: he had realized that not even then—the happiest day in his life, when he could see the near future but, vai!, not for Pașadia, for whom the lilies were already smiling—not even then would we accompany the dear man to the Arnoteanus, the true Arnoteanus. And why not? We had no idea how special it was, there was no party sweeter: a little poker, little maus, some chemin-de-fer, where could you always find them? The Arnoteanus. A little drink, a shpritz, a cognac, some Turkish coffee with a bit of rum, where? The Arnoteanus. A quiet girl, as cute and easy as your heart's desire, where? The Arnoteanus again and only with the Arnoteanus, the only true, blessed boyar family, adorned with every Christian virtue. To be direct: the Major was a monkey, but Cucoana Elvira, what a woman! and the girls, they were pussycats, pussywillows. Ah, if we wouldn't go, we must want to hurt him, to embarrass him, and that was not very nice of us, not how you treat a brother. And he fell to pieces. Hiking his shirt over his face, he cried bitterly.

Even if he had been sincere, and he was, in a manner of speaking, he merited none of our sympathy. If he could not hit his cheap target, the fault was his alone: well he knew that we would go anywhere with him; on nights out with Paşadia, the three of us followed blindly, what would have been easier than taking us there without asking or even telling us ahead of time? Maybe the thought had passed through his mind, it would have been like him, but he was afraid. To see us with the Arnoteanus, after our unyielding opposition ever to set foot in that place of gambling and fornication, seemed so impossible to him that he felt like the toy of fortune when he saw that it was enough for me to casually suggest, apropos of nothing, "What if tonight we stopped by the true Arnoteanus?" for Pantazi to say, "Why not?" and Paşadia that there was as good as anywhere. Gorică did not simply go mad with wonder or happiness; he went completely into fits, he howled, flopped on the ground, rolled about, and we had to threaten to change our minds before he gave up the idea of riding there on the backs of the hansom-cab horses.

That I don't know the name of the street where the Arnoteanus lived should not seem strange; for the month I attended religiously, I never had occasion to enter or exit except through the unfenced end of the courtyard, which gave onto the right quay of the Dâmboviţă, up a little from Str. Mihai Vodă. It was nearer, and no one would see me.

My first visit is an unpleasant memory. I experienced an hour of self-exprobration in which I upbraided myself for entering this sewer. Lord, the people I congregated with that evening, the number of handshakes I endured! Paşadia's bitter remonstrance resounded, unforgiving, in my ears. The evening would have been unhappy if it had only been dull; Pirgu's high spirits had vanished, now he played the "boss," he knocked card tables together, pulled chairs over. He put Paşadia into a game of poker, Pantazi in chemin-de-fer, and women on the right and left of both. In the silence that precedes the first blow, from the unillumined chambers that gave onto the large room in the middle, came whispers, muffled laughter, a sigh.

I determined it was the right moment to split, English-style; they wouldn't catch me a second time. I thought I had escaped when, in the doorway, I came face to face with "Mother Soul," Cucoana Masinca Drângeanu.

"You're trying to escape walking me home," she said, holding out her tiny, gloved hand palm up, so I could kiss the bare skin above her wrist. "You don't love me anymore . . ."

"I will permit you, my dear cucoana," I interrupted her, "to think me capable of many injustices, but not that!" It was not artless flattery on my part; was it truly possible not to go crazy for her?—and not because of the beauty she retained in spite of her age, which she cheated as she had the two men she married and the many she had not, but because she had a "come hither" air impossible to resist in all of her motions, her voice, her eyes. I naturally reconsidered my departure and became the witness to an unusually warm welcome, even for the country of Romania. The mistress of the house and both her girls pounced on the newly arrived woman and attempted to outdo each other with embraces and kisses. All at once they pestered her, without pausing for her to respond, with questions about Nice, from where she had just returned; they caressed her, admired her, they insisted she have a drink. As much out of pity as anything, "Mother Soul" decided on coffee, then let herself be persuaded to add a Cointreau. She refused to be the fourth in a game of maus, and she alighted beside me at a table beside a mirror, in which we could see all of the games in the neighboring salon.

She wanted to know why I was in a hurry to leave—perhaps I had a rendezvous? I didn't hide the truth. She admitted I was partly right: Did I think she enjoyed associating with Frosa Bojogescu or Gore Pirgu? But what was there to do? It's like this everywhere there's gambling, and she lived off what happened after the game. Should I judge her for this, when I had the pleasure of knowing the Arnoteanus?

Of course she didn't mean the Major: he was such an idiot! Still, he had his good points: a strength of character which, no matter what, was impossible not to admire. Dirt poor, in debt to his ears, rejected by a family who did not want so much as hear of him, avoided by the upstanding, booed and pointed at, he was unflappable, he maintained his pride, his demnity, his hauteur. Unperturbed by all that did not touch him directly, neither his wife nor his daughters interested him in the least; he might see them perish before his eyes without shifting his weight from one foot to the other, he would happily have worn gloves sewn from their skin. As his worthy off-spring, the girls would also have made his tough leather into purses, pretanned and waterproof. In contrast, his wife still loved him desperately, she loved like a martyr, she served like a slave, taking care after care—oh, some of them so revolting—she coddled him, kept him, although well she knew that their "little Major," as they called him, visited other women, not exactly high-born women, and would come home without a dime and even sometimes battered, scratched, and bruised. So, it seems, had happened that very day: he didn't gamble, he stomped around longing to, and kept touching his eye, which sported a healthy lump. I watched him in the tilted mirror, the self-proud abortion circling the gaming tables with his short steps, the wizened Gypsy rising onto his toes, lifting his wrinkled and withered face over the kibbitzers' shoulders; I watched him, searching in vain for any trace of the decorated officer whose yellowed photograph was on the table, handsome and sured as he was when the barber Coriolan put him on the list with the phrase "piccolo, ma simpatico." Demonstratively, his callousness did him as little service as it did siccicate half the love out of his girthful wife. Still young in her face, tubby and pale, she energetically marched her sagging plumpness among the guests; swaying her fallen breasts and aged thighs, she joked and laughed, gave each person a word and a smile. Yet one could perceive in her a veiled sadness, which I hastened to ascribe to her unfaithful husband and unbridled daughters. Masinca did not let me remain puzzled for long: Elvira was not foreign to her daughters' downfall, and as far as the infidelity was concerned, for all the love in her heart, she had let herself be outdone, she kept up with the Major, even if she had given him a head start. If she did feel unsatisfied, no cause would ever be found. At the Arnoteanus' home, there might be days without bread, but none without an argument, but the yelling would be nothing if that were all it was, instead the girls fought and scrapped, they pelted each other with whatever they had at hand, clawed and bit and tore their clothes, and then both of them came running to their mother, and then they beat her to a pulp. Their screeching made their neighbors startle and passersby run off. But the Major? . . . The Major, "the abortion"—that's their name for him—he stayed away, he only steps in if the joke gets out of hand, then he runs outside and in his nasal voice calls for the "mpoleese." But look what happened to the poor guy: to celebrate May 10th, he donned his dress uniform only to find himself decorated head to toe with marinated meatballs. Over the year since the Arnoteanus had been renting from her—and the rent was an issue—Masinca did not have any need for the theater, and often she did not know whether she should laugh or cry. Ah! The girls were extraordinary, a thing of horror.

The older one especially, Mima. Always quick to tell you to call her "dear lady." She was only fifteen when, in Galaţi where her father was garrisoned, she turned the heads of two young men at once— gudgeons, both of them. Demanding constant proofs of their love, she asked one of them, the only child of wealthy parents, to steal some of his mother's jewelry, while she drove the other one, who worked as a cashier for a wholesaler, to spend far beyond his means, and, it appears, the mope stuck his hand in the till. Things didn't take long to come to light, and the boy from the good family, out of shame, blew his brains out, while the one from the store was tossed into prison for a year. The story came to a bad end for everyone but her. It snipped the thin thread that kept the Major in the army; the guilty girl was proud of her victory, and her satisfaction was justified, since her triumph was largely due to her power over men, though she could only turn their heads, not keep them. Masinca's well-intentioned attempts to set her straight had come to nothing: Mima was not some shepherdess who would toss an apple and run to cower behind the trees, our ancient and eternal school of flirting; for her, the charm of waves rolling murderously slowly, one after another, the subtleties of love, those little games of temptation and desire, stale yet never mistaken, were just pretensions and passé follies. Aggressive and game, if she spied a man she would growl and leap at his throat, and if she happened upon one who possessed the angelic strength to not run off in fear, she might leave some meat on his bones, but she also left him no reason to see her a second time. And Masinca artfully and most politely revealed that, due to a cruel trick of fate, this grown girl, well built even if a bit of a butcher, was not a complete woman; a kind of fault in her stitching from birth prevented her from healthy and complete couplings, and perhaps this had translated into her bent for couplings against nature, which made her lose even the little good sense she enjoyed; when she hooked up with a girl, she didn't shy from any shortcomings, any embarrassments, just the opposite: as cheap as she was, she didn't let costs get in her way, she'd take her around in a cab, buy her silk shoes, bottles of perfume; last summer, she and Rachel Nachmansohn tore through four thousand lei, money snagged from one Haralambescu while he was sleeping off a drunk at her place. She told the story herself; the way she talked you're ashamed to ask how she keeps food on her plate; at night she pulls the blinds up and strips all the way down, and when the priest visits on the first of the month, she comes to the door buck naked. Eh, what can you say, with everything and everything, with all her faults, a badmouther, a bedjumper, a bankbreaker, a blabbermouth, and a flake, who says and does everything upside-down and backwards and above all dangerously, ready to get you in trouble, still Mima had her fun side, she was nice enough, something you could never say about her younger sister Tita, who was as thick and dull as the other was sharp and lively, and aside from her immorality, lies, and meanness, she had nothing in common with her, except the filth—ah! hard to imagine and harder to describe their condition: after a certain hour, especially when it was hot out, you couldn't get near them for the smell; when they stood up they left a mark. After an illness in infancy, Tita ended up a little retarded, problems with her hearing made her meaner, and she was already cruel and nasty; people avoided the willow she was, and some of the gamblers complained she was a cooler. Even though she wasn't one to tell anyone no, she would only pull her skirt up in the dark; outwardly, in public, she carried herself like she was one of the chosen, something she sure didn't learn from the soldier who raised her; you'd never see her being cheeky or saucy, or hear her swearing or cursing at anyone. But the vast difference between the two was their build and appearance. Wide, weighty, and whitish, obviously destined for obesity in the near future, Mima was snub-nosed, with small green eyes under a single straight eyebrow, her forehead covered by uncombed puffs of chestnut hair, while Tita, small and svelte, with delicate, narrow wrists and ankles, carried her head wedged in between narrow shoulders, like an old phanariot who founds a church; she had brown, almond-shaped eyes, a long, aquiline nose, and shapely, thin lips. They had one thing in common: voices of a striking beauty. Each with her own stamp, but both fluid and clear; their singing reminded you of soft murmuring waters mimicking the whisper of the wind in the branches, and its charm was perhaps not alien to the pity I felt, hearing those sad stories. Here was the proof, in flesh and bone, that old, fallen families committed a grave sin, in their depravity, by failing to follow a Malthusian logic and getting spayed, before it was too late. Think how much suffering and pain they would be saved . . . Mother Soul's departure left her arrival nothing to envy for tenderness. With tears in her eyes, the lady Major assured me that she would never find a second friend like her as long as she was alive. I wanted to say it would also be needless. But when Masinca was outside the doorway and I was still inside, someone placed a gloved hand on my back. It was Mima. Puckishly indicating my fellow traveler, she flashed an all-too-eloquent gesture with her middle finger and dashed away laughing.

Exiting into the yard, I noticed the inquination of the Arnoteanu house, including the building where they slept. To a square, one-story building had been added a slanted, narrow tail with two floors, a ragged gallery left unplastered and windowless spanning from one end to the other and giving onto the kind of tower, all planks and scrap mending plates, that housed the stairs. This ruin, which by day would have passed unnoticed, acquired, under the lunar brightness, a mysterious air, and as I stopped to ponder it, a chill shivered through me. From inside came one long, lugubrious cry, a howl that did not seem canine.

"They brought the old woman back," said Masinca. "The Major's mother."

The poor thing, God had not pity enough to take her. She didn't even know her own name, now that she had lost her mind. The least they could do would be to leave her in peace and not toss her about, here and there. Her daughter, the wealthy Princess Canta, from Moldavia, the Major's half-sister, was sometimes put in his care, though she would never stand for it, and sometimes was taken back to her home; why? it remained to be seen, the princess was somehow strong-headed about her musicians. The Major was only waiting for one thing: to get his mother's stipend he would have even had a Mass said for her, not because he missed her—he barely knew her—but he had picked up a few coins the past months—out of the princess's pocket—and the poor thing was no burden: he had the room and she didn't need to be watched; she didn't do anything wrong; in fact, she didn't do anything at all, she didn't make a sound, didn't move, she stayed balled up like a roly-poly at one end of her bed; but on nights when the moon shines, even if the blinds are down, she will climb out of bed and crawl around and howl, as I had heard. And you'd give a lot not to see her . . . the specter.

She still lived, although forgotten, the storied Sultana Negoianu; as though reincarnated, re-created by some curse, the haughty Amazon had been condemned to survive, she who in a short time had succeeded, as was not exactly easy to do at the time, in horrifying the as yet un-united principalities with her opulence. I knew her past, I had researched the enigmatic, disturbing smile that beckoned from her portraits—the stormy past that had made the name of her family into a curse, that great line of which she was the sole remaining descendant—I had researched its history, as though I had known that the chance to transcribe it would become mine. She had been raised in Geneva and Paris, whence she returned to the country at the age of sixteen, with a mode and high manner that surprised the chattering people. Her imposing dowry decided the great Minister Barbu Arnoteanu, without further thought, to ask for her hand. The marriage was turbulent and brief; still recovering after delivering the boy who would become the Major, the dear lady ran off with someone to Moldavia, where Iaşi admired her just as much as had Bucharest, she waved tirelessly through balls, she passed by proudly on a galloping horse, pursued by a flock of enthralled admirers. The gift of two estates convinced her abandoned husband to consent to their divorce, and she married the one-time Great Logothete Iordachi Canta, a Russian prince and unhappy candidate for the rule of Moldavia; this union was even less destined to survive than the first: life with an invidious and avaricious husband in the wildly lonely palace in Pandina, lost among the wizened forests on the banks of the Prut, could not have held any charm for the incendiary Sultana, who departed just after the arrival of their daughter Pulcheria, without his knowledge and without a thought of return, for Bucharest. At the price of another two estates, she found herself on her own feet, and she had no desire to bind them again. She lived. As magnanimous with her body as she was with her wealth, as though the prey of an annihilating rage, she had herself ravished, royally, and still unsated, she fouled herself with dogs. I will limit myself to noting the concord between this passion and her earlier, not infrequent outbreaks, which did not delay in returning. One autumn morning in 1857, she was found wandering with her hair down and her clothes off around the lake in Herăstrău Park. Ah, yes, I was forced to admit: when he said that if I wanted material for a novel I need not go farther than the true Arnoteanus, Pirgu did not deceive me.

He was the first one I encountered, following that evening. On the boulevard in front of Eforiei, he blocked my path. He held his hands out, one cupped in the other, both palm upwards, his thumbs sticking out and slowly writhing.

"Long may you live, Lord Scalyfish!" He made an Oriental bow. "You're one of us. Don't you know how to spew your milt where it matters. You were writhing on Masinca's fishline, weren't you, little by little you rubbed your sweet rosin on those strings. You're such a brat, amice, you pretend like you're a rooster, like you're a tomcat. Eh, you still have a lot to learn; you're not a bull, you're a bull calf. And if you want to please the monkeys, you have to be a hog, with a fatty rind. Whatever you do, don't yank yourself dry; if you smell defeat, push your donkey a little further down the road; you know the saying, we need a bull because the pond is full of frogs. If you see her tail go up, don't be shy, hold it out at the right angle, go in like a ram, and by winter your carp will grow fur."

"That," I told him, "is the thanks I get for making your dream come true, when I walked in to the Arnoteanus' house, before your very eyes?"

"After you'd led me down the path for six months. And if you did go, whose was the triumph, mine or yours? Good Lord, you left with the dame and they all went belly-up, one after another; Pantazi never saw so much cash since the day his mamma made him. But what to do, everyone's got their own kind of luck, and yours is better than anyone's. Touched by God, you are."

The indifference with which I listened did not discourage him.

"You like her a lot, don't you, and she's not your usual type. Hell if I know what she sees in you. She insisted I put a word in for her."

I was not curious. I assured him only that I had no desire to increase the number of intellectuals who abused the gentility of Dr. Nicu.

"Ah!" he grinned, "you can't hide from that, you can't escape. It comes when you're not looking, some evening along the road, you take a schickster home and then it's on the sheets. Why shouldn't the scripture be fulfilled: 'He will descend in the form of a bird'? Why be so scared? By my reckoning, it's better to get it over with, do it right, adieu worries: you can't get it twice. Then you're on your way. You're going to bring up the other one, but for that there's a cure. So why let a little thing like that keep you from the sweetest thing in the world? What else do you want from life?"

"You're completely right," I admitted. "Good-bye."

"What's the hurry? Is Masinca waiting?"

"Maybe later. At the moment, I'm looking for Pașadia and Pantazi."

I wasn't lying: they had been missing for three days. Pașadia was no surprise, perhaps he had gone to the mountains—but Pantazi?

"Well, if you want to find them," said Gore, "come with me."

"Where?"

"Eh, bravo. You have to ask? At the Arnoteanus, the true Arnoteanus."

What surprised me was not the fact they were there, but the detail that the one who had wanted to return, and desperately, was Pantazi. What was the attraction? Gambling was out of the question; he wasn't a gambler and even if he were, what could that flea-sized game mean for one of his enormous means? Women? But in the nine months since we, becoming friends, lived so close, I knew of no affair, no caprice no matter how fleeting—once when our conversation turned to those dolls that, I had heard, sailors use in place of their wives on long journeys, he assured me that this disgusting deviancy was no fairy tale: they were available on demand or made to order to particular resemblances; the expensive, Dutch ones attempted to re-create living beings in every way. Without my wanting, the thought crossed my mind that perhaps the dear man was hiding a doll of his own, in one of the capacious coffers stacked in his bedroom, one that precisely reincarnated his unfaithful and unforgotten Wanda. And if not women, then what else had made him renounce the solitude of the best flowers of Bucharest? I never discovered the bait destiny used, in these surroundings, to reach its goal.

As for me, I should be grateful. A very long life would never have shown me all the baseness of which the human soul is capable, as did those five weeks I lived at the Arnoteanus'. Their house was a combination of a way station and an inn, a brothel, a gambling house, and a madhouse, was wide open any time to anyone, the meeting place of all the cursed and inquinate of our time: professional gamblers and provocateurs, drifters, stumblers and the fallen, the broken and the broke, ravaged by the taste for a life without work and above power, willing to sate their desire by any means, those whose methods were unrevealed or unclean, those outside the ranks of work or the ranks of men, some who had been to prison already, some who were on their way; and then there were the even more revolting women: baize hags at the green table, somnolescent and dour, their hands trembling over their money and cards, young women demarried at least once and soured by abortions and disease, on the prowl and on their guard against both sexes' various schemes and ever-changing alliances and dalliances, separations and enmities. A rancid haze of vice weighed like a fungus over the miserable décor—everything there was to see, in the seductive light filtered through crepe rose lampshades, was not only ugly and cheap, but also kept from the sun, stained with wet, dusty and smoky, devoured by termites or moths, stubby or skew, chipped, torn or mismatched—and this mess urticated and irritated Pașadia even more than the Major who would buttonhole him, drive him mad with the Arnoteanus' genealogy, claim to be greater than Brâncoveanu, among whose highest-ranking knights, as historians had proven, his family had numbered before they rose to the rank of boyar. The poor Major did nothing but highlight his own stupidity, because if he wanted to brag about his family, it would have been simple to do so with his mother's side, a truly great family and ancient for Wallachia, raising its Craiovan line without obstruction or hesitation up to the mid-fifteenth century, from great-ban to great-ban, intermarrying with only the most illustrious voivodes. Stupid he certainly was, but also noble: he who were it not for his parents' wastefulness would have been the flattered and pampered master of great wealth, and would have been, naturally, at least a royal adjutant-general and vice-president at the Jockey Club, but, vai! having become what he was, he did not breathe a word of regret, complaint, or jealousy, carrying within—since not feeling it was impossible—his mourning for his house and rejecting, with cheeky scorn, both ridicule and compassion. Furthermore, he was good to the lowly and quick to pity, yet not as quick as his wife, a Leliwa, from the proud Polish family, who could not look dry-eyed on any suffering, always ready to take the food from her own mouth or the cloak from her back. Certainly, weighing in the balance both good and bad, may we say that neither one of them deserved their fates.

I went to the Arnoteanus at first with some embarrassment, because I was treated with an importance out of proportion to the expense I could bear. As I suspected, this was due to a few lies about me planted by Pirgu: he said that Pașadia and Pantazi held me quite dear, one being my uncle, the other my godfather. How could I not be received with open arms by everyone in the house, how could they not treat me better than anyone else—when our arrival opened the sluice of a river of gold? This time, the Major had not even realized his mother had again been taken off to Moldavia. I do not know how I managed to miss seeing her, and I was sorry. Defeated was I not, however. There was another person, just as strange, in spite of her tender years.

A girl who reminded me of long, pallid stalks of celery grown in the dark, in sand, a mute girl. Mute because she was deaf?—but then her hearing must have been replaced by another sense, because she started at the softest sound, turning in question toward the source. She bore a striking resemblance to that small and boney Prussian princess whose wax bust smiled through the windowed cabinet door at Monbijou; the same insipid, elderly face, the same sharp features, the same cruel eyes. Lonely, unused to people, she would run and hide if you meant to touch her. When I asked Pirgu what ailed her, he said that, in the style of Lot, apparently, the Major had made her with one of his girls when he was drunk. Without taking the presupposition that far, it suggested to me the possibility she had spent some time under the same roof as her great-grandmother and great-grandfather. Not long after the old woman was taken away, the girl also disappeared.

The exceptional esteem I enjoyed with the Arnoteanus did not protect me from paying Mima tribute; to avoid it, I made use of all types of hazards and ploys, some of them patently false, to forebear and prorogue. One afternoon, when we happened to find ourselves alone, I thought my ship was sunk.

She invited me to her room, where, as though she were about to bathe, she despoiled herself of what little the dear woman had on. I expected she would tell me to do the same, but she only asked, in passing, if I thought she looked good. And with determination, she swiftly pinned up her hair, put a little white here, some red there, and dressed herself again from head to foot. I could not believe that uncinctured wild woman was the same punctilious beauty I led down the street a quarter hour later, on my arm. Yet so it was: at home, a soiled shirt right against her skin, her ragged skirt twisted to one side, and shoeless, in felt slippers, but when she went out—as she seldom did—she would be beautifully done up, maybe a little boyish, her gloves always fresh, her lacquered boots untouched by her well-pulled stocking, and in the best hansom one could find.

With me, however, she walked, slowly, taking obvious detours, talking, only her talking, without thread or plot, jumping from one thing to the next, mixing everything up, saying nothing of any significance. We arrived in front of Paşadia's house, which, in the dusk, appeared to glow fantastically from within. She studied it a long time, she asked in detail about its layout, the furniture, the servants, addressing a long list of questions to me, whose point I did not understand until the last one arrived, with stunning effect: Could I imagine she might ever become my aunt? She had seen Paşadia, he was the man she needed, she wanted to take him as her husband . . .

—had we then been the friends we would later become, I would have told her plainly to perish the thought. I met Paşadia later than I did Pantazi; in a word, while the latter could be ferociously condescending and beguiled by the most infantile prejudices, the former, when needed, was just as cunning a businessman as his loanshark uncle, and a pander no less frightening than his learned father. No, Paşadia would sooner lose his head than take such a step, and then, there was the fact that he did not like Mima; he found her boring and tiresome, while he did have feelings for Tita, whose nature matched his own: Did she not resemble one of those untamable predatory birds that, when mortally wounded, with both wings broken, gathered their last powers to hurl themselves, one final time, against their conquering enemy? I had once shared some of Paşadia's opinions about Mima, but soon I found them unfair; she was a sick creature, of course, lost, and dirtier, meaner, and more dangerous even than Masinca said she was, but pleasant enough and close, as tempting and sweet as sin itself, as graceful and lively as light on the waves. Now hounded by hopelessness, now by the wildest happiness, just when you thought she had been battered down, suddenly, unexpectedly, she grew stronger, rose up, somehow haughty and liberated; even her appearance would alter: sometimes slouched and jaundiced, with glassy, half-closed eyes, in the next moment she was tall, ruddy, and fresh, with moist lips, her gaze like dewfall. Her constant variation endowed her infirmities with a certain charm, the woman was ever desired and never possessed, like those fairies of the mist, daughters of the air and water who could never be embraced by mortals. Ah, no, those two poor bastards did not pay too dear a price, one his honor and the other his life, for the joy of knowing her . . .

. . . and she begged for my support to bring her plan to fruition.

I vowed to apply myself completely, but at the same time, I alerted her that the one who enjoyed decretory influency over Paşadia was not I, but Pirgu. I saw her explode in laughter, under the blue-beaded veil. I knew that between the dear woman and Gore there had once been something that left neither the one nor the other satisfied. In public, they acted the best of friends; when they saw each other, she would start with, "Nene Gore lookin' good, as hard in the saddle as he is on foot," and he, his hand on his heart, would be all deference, calling her, "Her highness, her greatness, her luminescence," he would offer to spread a rug for her feet and to sell himself as her Oriental slave; when their backs were turned, he was nothing but a dickwad cocksucker, she sent him to the madhouse and the salt mines, and he insulted her with fire and brimstone, she was a stinking, piece-of-shit paparuda, and he prayed to God to not lame his legs before he danced like a maniac, at least once, on her grave.

"Eh," Mima shrugged, "at the end of the day, if I have to, I'll make up with Pirgu."

It would have been difficult, because Gore was taking a break from the Arnoteanus. He had cleared up the question of his inheritance in the happiest way, selling it to an in-law at almost double the price he had hoped, and this brought about a profound alteration in his life. He had entered the year of the monkey, which could also be said of me, who once was careful to avoid him and now followed him about.

It was pure theater. When we ran into each other, I pretended to be in a rush. He asked me where to, and my response was always the same, "To the Arnoteanus, the true Arnoteanus."

He became angry: "You're on her like a hawk on meat, I took her in and left her for dead. Vous devenez agaçant avec vos Arnoteano; and you can go . . . Voyons, il faut être sérieux." Aside from the autochthonous Romanian insults whose deployment remained dear to him, he would only speak to me in French, and as loudly as possible, so everyone would hear. When I saw him coming down the street with one of his cucoanas, I slipped to the other side; if I knew the woman, I would duck into an entryway, around into a courtyard. And he, letting her pass on, would shout full-throated, "Regardez, mon cher, quelle jolie femme, comme elle est jolie, elle est jolie comme tout!" Once the cucoana was farther away, I would come back. He greeted me indignantly: "Mais, mon pauvre ami, ne soyez pas idiot; vous êtes bête comme vos pieds!" He'd walk off ahead of me, with his wide gait; after a few steps he would stop and put in his monocle, he would seem to take the measure of something high up on the house with the tip of his cane, then he would come back toward me, with a huff and a shrug: "Mais voyons, voyons." There always followed a pass through some shops to haggle over furniture, for the house he was thinking of building in the Romanesque style, and through the flea market for some icons; he bought all he could find; after a few such days, an entire wall of his hotel room, on Piața Victoriei where he had moved, was covered from top to bottom with immaculate misshapen women and spindly saints, including, among others, an unforgettable Saint Haralambie, olive-colored and wild, standing on laurel wreathes. But this could not compare with something that, if I had cared for him more, would have been cause for concern, something unbelievable and yet true: Pirgu was buying books. Easy to imagine what went through my mind when I saw him with four nicely bound volumes under his arm and I read the name "Montaigne" on the spine.

"What in the world," I exclaimed, "made you buy Montaigne?"

"Eh," he said, with a tender smile, "you know, Montaigne, he's nice, he has his parts." This was how he spoke sharing his opinions with his new friends, well-known lawyers or university professors, people on the move, with a future; he never gave his old gang another thought; he pretended not to know them. For me it was a singular experience to visit the locale where Pirgu enjoyed a fine midnight repast, while packs of the worst, the most evil, of Bucharest were clustered at the tables around him.

"What's with that guy?" they asked each other.

"He's English. Say whatever you want, he can't understand." And they would insult him, from across the room, behind a pillar, under the tables, they would shout at him, "Gore, Gorică!" But he, unmoved, as though he were not their target, ate and drank and lit his expensive cigarettes with the more pleasure the choicer their words.

Although he had pulled strings for invitations to join two important clubs, Pirgu ate at his native establishment every day, in order to show off his money—he always had it on him—and to run into Paşadia, with whom he was not speaking, just to look down his nose. Sawing away at this and that, he once happened to win a pretty sum. Instead of simply finding his dear friends, the future ministers, and listening to their talk about Bergson and the Hague Convention, Pirgu stubbornly pursued his defeat. Irritated by Paşadia's cutting coldness, by the grins and stinging barbs of those he had offended, he went on tilt, he gambled without rhyme nor reason, and he lost, lost everything—a fortune. Before dawn, Paşadia, who had taken the gross, withdrew, leaving him to the metal mending plates and falling debris. When, as empty and backward as his own pockets, he arrived home the next morning, he attacked Saint Haralambie; accusing him of bad joss, he pulled him off the nail and threw him through the window into the hotel courtyard. Whether he thought that he had provided our sinful age the miracle of an icon falling from the sky, I do not know, but something else happened which I admit I did not expect; I actually marveled; I would not have imagined such a parasite as he to have such strong and desperate drives. The very next evening, serene and reconciled with Paşadia, if not to his fate, Gore reappeared, ready for battle, at the Arnoteanus'.

One day when I went there with Pantazi, about noontime, we happened upon a girl unknown to us, who, with one bare foot resting on a chair, sang softly as she darned a stocking. When we entered, she raised her head and blushed to the whites of her eyes. I noticed Pantazi, too, was pale as death, his hand over his heart. "My God," I heard him whisper, "she looks just like her!"

This was the way I met "Miss" Ilinca Arnoteanu. I knew they had another daughter, their youngest, who had been taken from the cradle and raised, in Piatra-Neamţ, by the Major's widowed sister, stinking rich and childless. Ilinca's sixteen comfortable years passed in the peace of that romantic mountain nook, with its mysterious vistas that must have reminded her of the good knights who gave the estate its name, their sweet Suabie. The nickname that Mima gave her "new" sister, "Fräulein," fit her, not only because the place she came from was named for Germans, but also because of her looks. The gentle Moldavian sun had pardoned the dull straw of her braids and the ivory of her skin, both almost unnaturally pale; naked, I think she would glow in the dark. Her parents could not be any prouder of the dear girl; Elvira never paused in praise of her beauty and the Major her hard work; unforced, unguided even, Ilinca was always top of her class and was even preparing to skip a grade—not for nothing did she carry the name of those wise and well-educated ladies, granddaughter of the Negoianu line, daughter of Petraşcu-Vodă; and as everyone knew, it had been the quill of an Arnoteanu, Enache the Second, that authored the start of the renaissance of Romanian letters. She sat all day with her nose in a book, her feet carefully hidden under a blanket, as though she were embarrassed by their small size. Lacking the playfulness typical for her age, she was revolted by laughter and jokes, and in her severe expression, which made her childish face seem harsh, one could read intolerance for what she saw happening around her.

I agreed to tutor a few subjects in which she believed she was weak. As time passed, speaking of one thing and another, the strength of her mind impressed me—how soundly she judged, and how clearly. When once I mentioned it was rare to find someone who studied, as she did, for pleasure, she countered that she studied not from pleasure, but need, in order to have a profession. —Why, would she not be rich? It was known she was her aunt's only heir, and that woman increased the capital of her fat pension each year, returning almost all of its pretty profit. —Certainly, but she averred that aside from the fact that an inheritance could also be lost, it also was not a disincentive to the pursuit of a profession, on the contrary. —Under her own name? —Why not? Work was no embarrassment; work ennobles. Under her own name, suitable as a "belferiţă" (that's the word she used for "tutor") she would be more appreciated and respected; this respect she prized more than anything else. How well she knew what was due to her name and what her name was due; its still-vivid prestige had been demonstrated to her before she had been aware. During an oral exam, a puffed-up district inspector, surprised by the responses from the little "pupil" Ilinca Arnoteanu, asked if she were not a member of the "historic" Arnoteanu family, and learning it was so, he began to call her "Miss" and found many flattering words to use for the dear girl, holding her up as an example. And when she went with her aunt to visit Mrs. Elena Cuza, their neighbor, why did she always want to sit next to her, in the place of honor?—because she was a "true" Arnoteanu. Yes, the great name of leaders, scribes, and founders, she would wear it with dignity; her sisters had done enough to stain it. Ah! those sisters, naturally she found them pitiful, but her pity was no impediment to chastising them bitterly. Why couldn't they control themselves, as she did, why did they not struggle against their nature? I also learned that, in spite of her pale external coldness—an icy bird's milk custard— her grandmother's incendiary blood had spoken early and clearly. Horrible feelings smoldered within her, she knew the pain of raw nights when her poor flesh seemed to unravel, rended by longing, she had been ill, thought she was going mad, but she would rather suffer anything other than opprobrium. Deciding, it seemed, she had revealed too much, she awkwardly changed the topic and asked if I thought she would pass both exams. With calm grandeur, I informed her she would pass neither one. Before the first, she would be married, and before the second, she would be no longer in the country.

It had been decided. The moment when Pantazi was so visibly struck by her resemblance to the afore-beloved Wanda, his old passion reawakened. His love, the only one of its kind, did not happen in stages, with germination first, then maturation; it burst out in a moment, it was demonic, obliterating, and Pantazi did nothing to protect himself, he let it penetrate as deep as possible, to the bottom, to envelop him in the voluptuousness of stoking its fire and suffering. He thought of the dear woman all the time, he spoke only of the dear woman, he begged me to tell of her, anything, even to insult her, as long as I spoke about the dear woman. And he drank. Although it was not more than usual—that would have been difficult—now he drank to get drunk, blotto; it took two tries to get him into his carriage. Late at night, he took me to sneak around the Arnoteanus' house; he would tremble as he approached his most-beloved's bedroom window. Whatever wonderful and well-fashioned things he thought to tell her, often very tender things, he would say them to me; her he avoided, and around her he would stutter, mumble something unintelligible and flee, afraid even to look at her. Owing he had as yet entrusted his secret to no one but myself, in the accentuated chaos of the Arnoteanus' house, it went unobserved. And doubtless it would not have gone any further, if I, led by the purest friendship for them both and sure that I was doing what was best, had not had the thought to unite them in marriage.

One evening, while he was still sober, as he began to blabber again about his great love for her, I told him plainly that I had my doubts. He just thought he loved; if it were true, by now he should be at least engaged. What was he waiting for, why not ask for her hand? I argued that he showed no appreciation for the fortune of having found again, after more than thirty years, the reembodiment of his phantom love, and this time, in a person of the same stripe as him. Yes, if it really were serious, not a moment would have passed before he placed his fortune at the feet of this charming girl, who had arisen from his twilight as clearly as the new moon in the light of the sun. And to think, above all, that Ilinca could soon become another's; with her beauty, name, and status, would she stay unmarried for long? At this, Pantazi, who until then had let me prattle on, contenting himself just to mock my words, suddenly shivered and awakened. I had struck the chord of jealousy in his heart, awakened the deeply human reaction that it is less painful to not have something than for someone else to have it, a woman especially. Ilinca's cause was thus won; the next day, I argued his before her. I held forth about my friend honestly and at length, I gave all the explanations, numbered the advantages that would come to her and her family from the match I proposed. She listened with her usual coolness, but she did not ask for time to think; she declared that if what I said regarding his wealth were only half true, she was ready to accept him. The acquiescence of her parents and aunt being as good as won, there was no danger of any further impediment; I was mistaken only in thinking that things would proceed in peace, without hitches; in other words, I reckoned as though there were no Pirgu.

Ever since he returned to the Arnoteanus, his pants seemed filled with nothing but ants. He left, he came, he went in and out of every door, it was as though he had multiplied. He brought in throngs of card players. He had developed a great affection for the Major, whom he would not leave alone; he called him honey, pecked his cheek, and it went straight to the Major's heart. They went out together at dusk and came back toward midnight, still together and all the more lively. He would only talk about the Major, he admired him so; we could not even imagine what a rake he was: he had driven a girl of fifteen out of her mind, a bonbon—a big girl—and he advised Pantazi, who dropped his gaze and made faces, not to fall behind because God wouldn't forgive him the way He had Paşadia. Soon, the Major would rue his easy conquest, and the same Gore who had provided her would put him under the care of Doctor Nicu.

But what was this scrofulousness in comparison with the thing he set rolling in secret, just like Ilinca's union, and at the same time. I heard it directly from Pirgu, over a froth of dreggish drink in the heart of the market, one morning after a night of distraction. Was he talking nonsense, or having me on?—because things like this, I thought, only happened in the feuilletons and yellow rags; I had forgotten we were at the gates of the Orient. Working under the assumption that women are nothing more than saleable goods, he saw in Ilinca goods of high value and set to work, the circumstances being in his favor. Every dime of the many ventured since we arrived at the Arnoteanus notwithstanding, they, passionately profligate, were tighter than ever before, awfully tight, while Paşadia, whose gambler's luck never abandoned him for a moment, had more money than he knew what to do with. Pirgu reckoned he could make great use of this combination of states, and he managed, with his customary internunciary perspicacity, to convince Elvira to sell her daughter, and Paşadia to buy her, for a price just as monstrous as the deed itself, the lion's share of which would go to Pirgu. Now I understood the purpose of the excursions we were planning to the convents at the outskirts of town; at one of them, where we were to be lodged overnight, a slightly drunk Ilinca would be left Paşadia's defenseless prey. To bring this contemptible plan to naught was, once I discovered it, a trifle, but I wanted to do so such that everything lay buried in silence and oblivion, as it would have happened if, the moment after we parted, Pirgu had not run into Pantazi and confessed everything. I was grateful that circumstances prevented my witnessing the next several hours' events. At the Arnoteanus, before the main meal, to which Pantazi had invited Pașadia, a commotion erupted from the salon, where they had remained alone for the aperitif; suddenly one heard howls, smacks, thumps, things being overturned and glass breaking, and I think that one can imagine without excessive effort the faces of those who, running in, saw Pașadia and Pantazi locked in the most hopeless battle, slapping, punching, kicking, rolling on the floor, now one on top, now the other. And Pantazi was the most disheveled and tawdry man who ever asked, as he did in the next moment, for the hand of a girl, let alone a true Arnoteanu.

I was informed of all of this by a still-dazed Pirgu, after I had received a missive from each warrior; both requested that, in expectation of a resolution through arms, I would serve him as a witness and secure a second. It was easier than I would have imagined to prevent them taking the field. I knew of the fear which, in spite of his rejection of the world, Pașadia had of its opinion, thus by depicting the decisive effect it would have on his renown as "monsieur," the public knowledge of the grounds of this "affair" which could be called anything except "of honor," I did not miss my mark, as neither did Ilinca by demanding, at my direction, as her first engagement gift, a renunciation of the duel. More than to my boredom, my mind had gone to the thought that Pașadia's hand might have been cursed enough to destroy everything for the poor girl. In the following moment the girl had written to invite her aunt in Moldavia. Instead of one aunt, however, she received two.

The great white and red flame was carried down from Pandina palace. With her retinue of, as she called them, "pure idiots" (a parrot, two dogs, and three cats) and "impure idiots" (a French domestic, an Italian groom, a Gypsy chef, and two musicians, Czech and German), Princess Pulcheria departed for Bucharest. Two days in advance, Dospinescu, her ancient seneschal, had four large hotel chambers vacated, in order to fill them up again with her pesterant encumbrance; he rented two Bösendorfer and engaged one carriage-man for the daytime and another for night.

The little excesses of a great cucoana. Others, even more blameworthy, could pass unnoticed because she was also a great artist. Her music salon in Paris, and especially the enlightened support many young artists found with the dear woman, those composers and virtuosos whose fame was later indisputably consecrated, had saved the name of Princess Canta from oblivion, designated her place of honor in the history of music in the second half of last century.

She was—I learned—Pantazi's oldest friend. In 1863, Cneaz Canta, arriving in Bucharest for diverse reasons, was hosted for a few months, together with his daughter, by Lady Smaranda, where the boyars crowded into the room to hear little Pulcherița at the virginal. The same age as ***, they lived there like sister and brother, and the memory of that time was sweet to them both, each preserving the image of the other as they were: she more mature and dark, bold and imposing, he blond and small, pious and impressionable. After his departure from the country, she was the only society person with whom he remained in contact; they wrote to each other, they met in Milan, Bayreuth, Paris. He had felt obligated, therefore, to inform her, immediately, that he had decided to take her niece as his wife.

He went out to meet her as far as Milcov. The lady barely recognized him in his new form, and the story of his change of name enchanted her. She was impatient to meet Ilinca. The long interview of aunt and niece resulted in something completely unexpected: at parting, the Princess, conquered, whose brief marriage—also with a Canta, from another branch—had been barren, swore a solemn oath to Ilinca that she would adopt her.

The happiness with which I received this piece of news was spoiled in part by another. To satisfy the other aunts, Ilinca decided the wedding would not take place during May, the month of Mary, which meant a delay of almost three weeks, a deeply unsatisfying turn for Pantazi. For some time he was constantly deep in thought, disquiet, unsettled.

One evening, he suggested we eat at his house, just us two. It was not to tell me anything significant. Late, leaving together, we climbed into a hansom that apparently happened to be at the corner, but was actually waiting for him; I noted that the carriage took us, without instruction, via a route unknown to me, outside the city. I was used to this kind of excursion; the year previous, it had often happened that, toward autumn, we would go to the countryside at night, to find a rise of earth where we could look for Fomalhaut shining through the broad band of the dawn. But on that overcast evening there were no stars or moon, the sky was completely covered, and yet you could see almost like it was day, every outline was distinct, the trees seemed to be glowing from within. At a clearing, Pantazi ordered the hansom to stop and suggested we walk. He led me farther on, where there arose a tumbled-down, roofless ruin.

"The Devil's Inn," said Pantazi. "Only here in Ilfov are there so many, all of them with their horror stories of bandits and ghosts. I once hosted a party here, at night, by torchlight."

I became aware that there was now a third; as though out of the ground, a Gypsy appeared, an old Gypsy woman in rags. After exchanging a few words with Pantazi in the Gypsy tongue, she sat on her heels and began to conjure, tossing rose petals onto a tray. Listening to her words, Pantazi's face turned to wax and his eyes shone like two blue beads. When the Gypsy stood up, he gave her a gold coin and we left.

"Strange," he murmured in a quiet voice, "she couldn't read anything in the petals, aside from a sign of death."

I hid my indignation that a person like this dear man would subscribe to such silly heresies. And I counted the days until the end of the month. I set off to deposit the marriage forms and to ask the Princess's lawyer to expedite the adoption papers. Ilinca's indifference to all this had begun to anger me as much as her insulting ways of acting toward those both outside and inside her family; I imagined that she was not sincere when, with a smile pulled from her grandparents' portraits, she said that if nothing came of this, all it would mean for her was a year lost from school, and she would go back to Piatra without remorse. She would not accept a small gift of jewelry from Pantazi, asking how could it compare with those from Lady Smaranda? She only asked him to buy her a camera. It was the tool of her fate's fulfillment. One morning, seeing an oddly dressed girl in the milkwoman's phaeton, Ilinca requested she be brought, so Ilinca could photograph her. Only just rising after a bout of scarlet fever, the girl transmitted the illness to Ilinca. It began so slightly that it seemed she would soon be back on her feet, but suddenly it acquired such force that, even with all the doctors in Bucharest, and one brought in great haste from Vienna, even with the million promised to the one who saved her, Ilinca perished.

On the very morning of her death, in a note of few words, Pantazi asked me to see to her burial. He could not know that what he was asking was beyond my powers. I needed help from someone, and I did not know anyone more skilled than Pirgu. Finding him was not easy. From Dușumea to Vitan, Geagoga to Obor, changing cab after cab, I set foot in every den I knew, one after another and some more than once, without finding trace of him. Of everyone I asked, only Haralambescu had seen him, earlier that evening at Moshi's, pig-drunk, with a barefoot girl, nine months pregnant. Around two in the afternoon, I gave up my search and decided I must gather my courage and fulfill the sad mission alone. But first, as I had not tasted a thing since the previous evening, and worried my exhaustion would soon overcome me, I entered the Capşa for a coffee and kirsch. And who should I spy? Gore, Gore Pirgu in the flesh. His face was as dark as his liver, and he swore in anger.

"I thought," I said to him, "that after your success last night I would find you somewhat happier."

He grinned wide. "It was 'di granda.' On my honor I thought she would calf right on top of me."

And while I sipped my coffee and kirsch, I told him what had happened. There was no need to ask him to take care of everything. I gave him free hand and had no cause for regret. Ilinca was interred royally, like Byzantine empresses; on the third day, the most beautiful day of May, we took her to her final rest, along with all the flowers in Bucharest. Notable at the burial was not the furious despair, perhaps remorse, of the aunt from Piatra, nor the parents' pain, surely doubled by the fact that along with their child they had lost their last hope of improving their fate, nor the shamelessly satisfied air of the sisters, who abhorred the departed and loathed her as much as she had scorned them—remarkable and worrisome was Pantazi's absence. Before Pirgu had finished his blessing, I went back into the city, more and more burdened by the thought that Pantazi had done himself harm. But passing by the low windows of the French establishment, through the open slats, I saw him at his usual table, in the furthest corner, eating and drinking quietly, with appetite. Since then, I have never set foot in the house of the Arnoteanus or ever mentioned Ilinca to him. It is as though she never was . . .

✦

. . . for three months Pantazi and I returned to the style of life we lived the previous year, meals that went on past midnight, sojourns until dawn through unfamiliar suburbs and down abandoned alleyways. The leaves sounded now like autumn, and just when the weather seemed it would settle, there were, as deep and heavy as never before, overwhelming fogs. Happening to sleep under the power of one of them, I had the most beautiful dream of my life.

In an old court, in the chapel of evil passions, the three Rakes, great-abbots of the most serene rank, celebrated their final service of vespers, silent vespers, vespers of the beyond. They wore long mantles, each with a saber at the thigh and cross on the breast, and aside from the scarlet of the heels, they were vested, bestoled, and enhusked only in gold and green, green and gold; I expected our earthly banishment would come to its end. A gentle song of bells announced that the Lord's spirit descended upon us; ransomed by our pride, we had to re-earn our high places. Over the priest's chairs, unseen bearers lowered banners with crests, and one by one all seven altar candles went out. And the three of us departed over a bridge toward the sunset, toward heavens ever more enormous in their emptiness. Ahead of us, in a manner of parti-colored buffoons, grimacing and grating, galloping and hopping, waving a black handkerchief— Pirgu. And we melted into the purple of dusk . . .

I was still under the impression of this dream when, entering the café, looking for news, I learned that Paşadia had died. His end echoed through the world, not because of his name, but by the way it happened. Recently, Paşadia, who was no longer seen anywhere, had been living with Rachel Nachmansohn. Everyone knew of the raw frenzy with which this person gave herself to a certain voluptuosity, and which justified the nickname "bloodsucker," given her by Gorică. Coming to rut over his voluntary prey, it had not taken Paşadia long to finish. Along with his last drop of manly power, blood spouted forth and his heart stopped beating. Worthy of her great ancestor Judith, little Rachel did not lose her presence of mind; she untangled her hair from the dead man's still-warm hands, dressed carefully and, untroubled, visited the police commissar and asked him to pick up the cadaver, which, with blessings from above, was done in silence—in these circumstances was there any point in a scandal?—such that, in the overflowing dawn, at his usual hour, Paşadia returned, for the last time, to his home. I flew there in an instant. As I approached the dwelling without happiness, over the trees in the flowerless garden, in the quiet of the evening, there rose a pillar of smoke. The faithful hand had done its duty; in his cruelty, the man accomplished after death the most genteel of crimes. I mourned the loss of the works but not their author. Paşadia had perished at his zenith; the venom, vigil, and vice had destroyed his body without damaging his spirit in the least; he preserved his cold clarity to the end, sparkling like a star in the crystalline sky of a frigid night. And he had been fortunate enough to die before being forced to endure for a second time, after the war, in old age, the humiliation of poverty; before suffering, what perhaps would have been even more galling, the bonfire of his disappointments and disproofs, to see that not he but Pirgu had been right, to see Pirgu himself a millionaire many tens of times over, married with a dowry and separated with a bribe, to see Pirgu prefect, member of parliament, senator, plenipotentate minister, presiding over a subcommittee on intellectual cooperation at the League of Nations, and offering his foreign colleagues, visiting Romania for fundraising or for an "investigation," a sumptuous and sybarite hospitality in his historical castle in Ardeal. I did not see Paşadia's body; when I arrived, they had already placed the seals, and the remains, according to his wish, had been quickly gathered and delivered by Iancu Mitan somewhere outside Bucharest, perhaps in "the mountains."

Pantazi, who had finally sold even the hovel on Bărăție, had nothing more to delay his departure. The night before, we dined together at the establishment on Covaci. Not far from our table, more beautiful and more impassive than ever, little Rachel presented her new fiancé, a type of toad with bulging eyes, broad and blunt. The musicians did not forget to play precisely that slow, dragging waltz Pantazi had a weakness for; voluptuous and sad, in its mollitious oscillation, it traced a nostalgic and endlessly somber passion, one so rending that the very pleasure of listening to it became a kind of suffering. When the taut violin strings began to mimic a careworn confession, the entire hall fell mute. Ever darker, lower, and slower, describing dolor and deception, wandering and pain, rue and regret, the song, suffocated in nostalgia, drifted away, withered into a whisper, to a lost, tardy, and pointless cry.

Pantazi wiped his eyes.

I wandered with the dear man, here and there, for the rest of the night, so we would reach the flower market at morning, in the Old Court. Alongside the fence of the church with a green tower, the pious flicker of a weak candle attracted us. Someone had left it burning by the head of a dead woman who lay modestly on a bed of leaves. If I had not been told, I would never have believed it was Pena Corcoduşa; how could I have recognized, in that soft face with delicate features, the frightening fury of last year? In the smile of her bruised lips and the gaze of her still-open eyes, there was an ecstatic tenderness; the woman who had been driven mad by love seemed to have died happy: perhaps in that short final moment that contained eternity, she saw her proud cavalier, whose being reflected the reunited glory of two royal weddings. That evening, I accompanied a gentleman to the border, he was clean-shaven, with short sideburns, in an elegant traveling suit—a foreigner. We sat in the restaurant car, face to face, and found nothing to say to each other. Night descended quickly. And I remembered that one who had ceased to be, the person who had seemed a friend since the beginning of the world and often another version of myself, I remembered Pantazi, when he asked what there was for us to drink.

These notes are meant as reading aids, rather than as a critical edition; they are a glossary for those wary of internet rabbit-holes that might interrupt enjoyment of the book. The translation is based on Barbu Cioculescu's edition of *Opere*, by Mateiu I. Caragiale (Bucharest: Editura Fundației Culturale Române, 1994). I also consulted a reprint of the 1965 Perpessicius edition (Bucharest: Editura tineretului, 1968). The list of critical works important to me includes: Matei Călinescu, *Mateiu I. Caragiale: recitiri* [Mateiu I. Caragiale: Rereadings] (Cluj-Napoca, Romania: Biblioteca Apostrof, 2007); Șerban Cioculescu, *Caragialiana* (Bucharest: Editura Eminescu, 1987); Cosmin Ciotloș, *Elementar, dragul meu Rache* [Elementary, My Dear Rache] (Bucharest: Humanitas, 2017); Alexandru George, *Mateiu Caragiale* (Bucharest: Editura Eminescu, 1985); and Ion Iovan, *Mateiu Caragiale: Portretul unui dandy român* [Mateiu Caragiale: Portrait of a Romanian Dandy] (Bucharest: Compania, 2002). Some information in the notes comes from pages Cosmin Ciotloș kindly provided me from Mateiu Caragiale, *Opere*, edited by Barbu Cioculescu (Bucharest: Univers enciclopedic, 2001).

Epigraph

v **Que voulez-vous, nous sommes ici aux portes de l'Orient, où tout est pris à la légère . . .** "What do you expect, we are here at the gates of the Orient, where everything is taken lightly . . ." According to the Romanian literary historian Perpessicius, the French statesman Raymond Poincaré (1860–1934), president of France from 1913 to 1920, made this comment in Bucharest while representing an Austrian company against the Romanian government in a suit regarding railway concessions.

Translator's Introduction

ix **Dressed in a green frock . . .** These details are drawn from George Călinescu's description in the second edition of *Istoria literaturii române de la origini pînă în present* [The History of Romanian Literature from Its Origins to the Present] (Bucharest: Editura Minerva, 1985) and Ion Iovan's biography, listed above.

ix   **"only for myself"**   "Ces notes je les écris uniquement pour moi" (Cioculescu [1994], 257).

ix   **memorized in full**   Ciotloş, 6.

ix   **even reenacted word-by-word**   Călinescu, 15.

x   **translated into a film**   *Craii de Curtea-Veche*, directed by Mircea Veroiu, with Ovidiu Iuliu Moldovan, Mircea Albulescu, Marius Bodochi, and Răzvan Vasilescu. Studioul de Creaţie Solaris Film [Solaris Film y Studio]—R.A. Cinerom / Studioul cinematografic „Bucureşti" [Bucharest Film Studio], 1995.

xi   **As Katherine Verdery observes**   *National Ideology under Socialism* (University of California Press, 1991), 21.

xii   **miraculous, massive, and apocryphal**   Ion Iovan, *Ultimele însemnări ale lui Mateiu Caragiale însoţite de un inedit epistolar precum şi indexul fiinţelor, lucrurilor şi întâmplărilor, în prezentarea lui Ion Iovan* [The Last Writings of Mateiu Caragiale, Accompanied by His Unpublished Correspondence, with an Index of Beings, Things, and Events, Presented by Ion Iovan], 2nd ed. (Bucharest: Curtea Veche Publishing, 2009).

xii   **picto-poem**   Mateiu I. Caragiale, *Craii de Curtea-Veche, cu ilustraţii de Răzvan Luscov* [Rakes of the Old Court, with Illustrations by Răzvan Luscov] (Bucharest: Humanitas, 2015).

xii   **reperformances**   In 2020, the Romanian division of the German supermarket chain Lidl launched a line of smoked meats under the slogan *"Te poftim la masa lui Mateiu Caragiale . . . Fii parte din poveşte"* ("We Invite You to Dinner with Mateiu Caragiale . . . Be a Part of the Story").

xiii   **French translation**   The French translation is the second of several complete translations of *Craii*.
Dutch: *Schelmen van het Oude Hof*, translated by Jan Willem Bos (Amsterdam: Uitgeverij Pegasus, 2019).
English: *Gallants of the Old Court*, translated by Cristian Baciu (Bucharest: Editura Paideia, 2011).
French: *Les Seigneurs du Vieux-Castel*, translated by Claude Levenson (Paris: L'Âge d'homme, 1969).

German: *Die Vier vom Alten Hof,* translated by Thea Constantinides (Bucharest: România Press, 2003).

Hungarian: *Aranyifjak alkonya,* translated by László Szenczei (Budapest: Európa Kiadó, 1966), revised by László Lörinczi as *Óvárosi gavallérok* (Bucharest: Kriterion, 1984).

Italian: *I principi della corte-antica,* translated by Mauro Barindi (Milan: Rediviva Edizioni, 2014).

Italian: *I Crai della Vecchia Corte,* translated by Florian Potra with Bruno Arcurio (Bucharest: Editura Minerva, 1980).

Serbian: *Starodvorske Lole,* translated by Vukosava Karanović (Belgrade: Nolit, 1977).

Spanish: *Los reyes de la Corte Vieja,* translated by José María Pallás (in *La configuración del espacio en la obra de Mateiu Caragiale,* PhD diss., Universidad Complutense de Madrid, 2003, https://core .ac.uk/download/pdf/19711002.pdf, accessed October 9, 2020).

Spanish: *Los depravados príncipes de la Vieja Corte,* translated by Rafael Pisot and Cristina Sava (Valencia: El Nadir, 2008).

xiv **the chapter that includes Mateiu** Călinescu, 897.

xiv ***Massachusetts Review*** "Rake's Congress" by Mateiu Caragiale, *Massachusetts Review* 55, no. 3 (2014), 481–94.

Rakes' Congress

3 **... au tapis-franc nous étions réunis.** The epigraph, "... we gathered at the dives," comes from Louis Protat (1819–1881), six-time president of the bacchic Société du Caveau and the author of erotic fiction.

3 **my good friend Uhry** Rudolf Uhrinowsky, a journalist and Mateiu's friend.

4 **Str. Covaci** A street in the center of Bucharest.

4 **Pantazi** Cioculescu (2001) finds records of the name in Wallachia going back to the medieval period, and a listing from 1895 for a partner in a law firm: "Cihosky—Pantazi—Procopiu." The four principal characters have names beginning with "p": Pantazi, Pașadia, Pirgu, plus the narrator, which in Romanian is "povestitorul." The number "four" starts with the same letter: "patru."

4　**ţuica**　Pronounced "tsueeka." A plum brandy, good before a meal to awaken the appetite—also good during and after a meal, or on its own.

4　**Paşadia**　The "ş" is pronounced "sh," and in both Romanian and English this name suggests the Ottoman title "pasha." Cioculescu (2001) finds many records of the name in Wallachia going back to the fifteenth century, including a Grand Logothete Radu Paşadia and, from a 1565 bill of sale, a Rom slave named Paşadia.

5　**precisely that waltz**　Ciotloş argues that Mateiu has a particular piece in mind, a waltz by the Romanian composer Iosif Ivanovici (1845–1902) entitled "Wanda."

7　**Podul Mogoşoaiei**　A major north-south artery in Bucharest leading toward Brâncoveanu's Mogoşoaia Place, renamed "Calea Victoriei" (Victory Street, see page 60 in this book) in 1878, thirty-two years before the setting of the novel, to celebrate Romania's independence from the Ottomans. This victory is a result of the Russo-Turkish War—the same that brings Prince Sergie Lichtenberg-Beauharnais to Bucharest.

8　**Benjamin**　In Genesis, Jacob's beloved youngest son, and Joseph's favorite among his brothers.

8　**Cherubino**　The lover in Mozart's *The Magic Flute.*

8　**gypsy**　The forms of "*ţigan*" that I have translated as "gypsy" (lowercase) are as pejorative in Romanian as they are in English, and just as normalized, e.g., "He gypped me out of a dollar." Where Mateiu uses it for particular people, such as the fortune teller, I have capitalized it.

9　**borviz**　A particular mineral water often mixed with wine.

12　**coliva**　A mixture of nuts, grains, and honey served at memorial services.

12　**licorice and jam**　That is, home remedies, palliatives for the dying.

12　**the Old Court**　A fifteenth-century castle and church located near the center of present-day Bucharest that was rebuilt in the seventeenth century by Constantin Brâncoveanu and ruined in the nineteenth (see the note to "Rakes," below). While mid-twentieth-century archaeological excavations uncovered much of the castle grounds and turned it into a museum, in Mateiu's time it was a ruin, the oldest in the city.

13 **Brâncoveanu . . . the columns at Hurez, the arcade porch at Mogoşoaia, the palace at Potlogi** Constantin Brâncoveanu (1654–1714), prince of Wallachia after Şerban Cantacuzino, was beheaded by the Ottomans and is known as a modernizer who brought the printing press and new ideas to Bucharest. Brâncoveanu is associated with an architectural style combining regional and Renaissance elements, one that enjoyed a revival at the start of the twentieth century. He founded the monastery at Hurez, near Făgăraşi, and built the palaces of Mogoşoaia and Potlogi, both near Bucharest. Ştefan Cantacuzino was his successor.

14 **cult of Comus** Comus is the Greek god of festivities, the son of Dionysus.

15 **Pena Corcoduşa** "Pena" is an old word for "punishment"; "corcoduşa" is the plum from which ţuica is made. In other words, her name means "hangover."

15 **rakes of the Old Court!** Pena's outburst, "crai de Curtea-veche," may have come to her because they meet near the Old Court ruins, but as Mateiu suggests, it is not her own invention. An archaic word for "king," sometimes used to refer to the Gospel magi (see page 33 in this book), the term "crai" circulated with some frequency in the nineteenth century, according to Cioculescu (1994), even in the construction, "crai de Curtea Veche." He asserts that Mateiu would certainly have known this passage from George Ionescu-Gion's 1899 history of Bucharest:

> The Russian-Turkish war between 1769 and 1774 was the coup de grace for the old Court. No one lived there anymore; in the vaults below and in the former guards' chambers, in the cellars and even in the attics above, all the filthiest people of Bucharest gathered, all the Greek adventurers took refuge here and made the glorious building of the old lords into a true *Cour des Miracles*. The Bucharest expression "Crai de Curtea-Veche" comes from this time. These vagabonds and charlatans so dangerous to the city were driven away and killed by a Turkish pasha called to Cotroceni [the new court] to help the merchants terrified of the thievery and banditry of the Crai de Curtea-Veche (131).

This is an ironic use of the term "crai" to denote a false, cuckoo nobility that debases the court. Mateiu literalizes this irony in his debased wealthy characters, mimicking the way the Old Court itself is ruined over time.

"Crai" is a difficult word to match in translation. My choice of the antiquated "rakes" attempts to suggest an aristocratic debauchery. The young, wealthy male seducers implied by "rakes" is close, my colleague Gabriella Koszta tells me, to "Alkony," the word used in the title of the first Hungarian translation. In another approach, a translator can rely on the word "court" in the title to provide the aristocratic valence and translate "crai" with debauchery alone. In this vein, an extended English fragment by Alistair Ian Blyth provides the delightful rendering, "The Old-Court Philanderers" (*Absinthe* 14, 2010). Bos tells me the word "schelmen" in the Dutch title is an old word for "rascals," and *schelmenroman* is the term for picaresque novels. One Spanish translation uses two words to express both senses: "The Depraved Princes of the Old Court," while the other Spanish translation, the French, and the more recent Italian translations reference only the nobility of "kings" or "lords" or "princes," leaving their debauchery to be discovered in the novel. Two translations avoid the word altogether: the German simply counts them, "The Four from the Old Court," and the earlier of the two Italian translations calls them "The Crai," a calque suggesting that the depravity signaled by the Romanian word is sui generis.

16 **Knights of the Bronze Horse**   "Les chevaliers du Cheval de bronze" were a group of Parisian criminals who would meet at the equestrian statue of Henry IV erected during the reign of Louis XIII, located in the Place de Vosges.

16 **the Muscovites found their Capua**   Capua was Hannibal's residence during the Second Punic War, a place of relaxation and luxury said to have softened his army.

16 **beautiful Sergei**   Sergei Leuchtenberg-Beauharnais (1849–1877) was the grandson of both Eugène de Beauharnais, Duke of Leuchtenberg, and Tsar Nicholas I, son of Maximilian de Beauharnais and Grand Duchess Maria Nikolaevna of Russia.

The Three Peregrinations

19 **C'est une belle chose, mon ami, que les voyages . . .**   "Travel, my friend, is a beautiful thing . . ."

19 **Sir Aubrey de Vere**   Sir Aubrey de Vere (1788–1846) was an English poet. Cioculescu (1994) lists several models for the character Aubrey

de Vere, who also appears in the novel *Remember* (Mateiu uses the English word), including Sir Aubrey's son, Aubrey Thomas de Vere, author of the book *Recollections*.

20 **Cișmegiu**   Older spelling of "Cișmigiu," a park in central Bucharest, consisting of an elegant network of bench-lined paths, with a shallow lake for rowboats.

20 **the comet**   Halley's Comet, which passes in May of 1910.

22 **Str. Modei**   A street that, before the bombing in World War II, ran behind the Royal Palace.

24 **the coming of spring at Ise**   The Ise Grand Shrine in Japan is the official temple of the Imperial family, dedicated to the sun goddess, Amaterasu.

25 **the beautiful Inês assassinated**   Inês de Castro (1325–1355), a lady-in-waiting to his wife, became the lover of Prince Pedro of Portugal. They lived together after his wife's death, in secret; her influence with the prince so threatened King Alfonso that he had her beheaded.

25 **the mad king died imprisoned**   Alfonso VI (1643–1683) was imprisoned for the last nine years of his life in a room in Sintra Palace in Portugal, where it is said his footsteps can still be seen.

27 **nene**   A term of affection and respect, used for a father or older brother.

27 **Govora**   A spa. Pirgu suggests he might pass Pașadia a venereal disease.

27 **Mărcuta**   An asylum for the insane, like the one that concludes William Hogarth's *A Rake's Progress*.

28 **a tale of Halima**   That is, as strange as something from the *Arabian Nights*.

31 **Suburra**   An ancient Roman red-light district.

31 **at Kehl with Berwick**   James FitzJames, Duke of Berwick (1670–1734) was a military leader, employed by Louis XIV, who led the siege of Kehl (today part of Germany) in 1733, during the War of the Polish Succession; he was decapitated the following year at Philippsburg by a cannonball.

31 **with de Coigny at Guastalla** François de Franquetot de Coigny (1670–1759), Marshal of France, was a commander at the Battle of Guastalla in 1734, during the War of the Polish Succession.

31 **the footsteps of Peterborough** Charles Mordaunt, third earl of Peterborough (1658–1735), was an English politician and military leader who took Barcelona in 1705 and died in Lisbon.

32 **le Bien-Aimé** Louis XV (1710–1774) was the king of France known as "Louis the Beloved."

32 **the feet of the Marquise** Jeanne Antoinette Poisson, Marquise of Pompadour (1721–1764), was an advisor and mistress to Louis XV; she died of tuberculosis.

32 **the philosopher of Potsdam** Frederick II (1712–1786), king of Prussia, was a prolific political writer known for spreading Enlightenment ideas of religious tolerance.

32 **Semiramis the Muscovite** Catherine II (1729–1796), empress of Russia, was a modernizer and supporter of Enlightenment ideas on governance, education of women, and the arts. She was called "the Great" and, in association with the mythical queen of Assyria, "Semiramis of the North."

32 **we allied with Belle-Isle at Frankfurt on the vote for Emperor** Charles Louis Auguste Fouquet, duke of Belle-Isle (1684–1761), Marshal of France, was sent to Frankfurt in 1741 to support the election of Charles Albert.

32 **we accompanied Richelieu** Louis François Armand de Vignerot du Plessis, duke of Richelieu (1696–1788), Marshal of France, was a philanderer, said to be the model for Valmont in *Les Liaisons dangereuses*, the French epistolary novel by Pierre Choderlos de Laclos (1782).

32 **Watteau canvases** Antoine Watteau (1684–1721), French painter.

32 **Elizabeth Petrovna** Elizabeth (1709–1762), empress of Russia preceding Catherine the Great, was a promoter of Enlightenment ideals and supported the creation of the University of Moscow. She forbade executions during her reign, including by decapitation.

32 **for Brühl** Heinrich von Brühl (1700–1763) was a politician at the court of Saxony and a confidant of the king. Lavish in his lifestyle, he owned Europe's largest collection of military vests.

33 **for Rameau** Jean-Philippe Rameau (1683–1764) was a French composer and the author of a *Treatise on Harmony*; he criticized the singing of the priest performing his last rites.

33 **and for Gluck** Christoph Willibald Gluck (1714–1787) was a Czech opera composer and the teacher of Antonio Salieri.

33 **Neuhoff** Theodor Stephan Freiherr von Neuhoff (1694–1756) was a German adventurer who was aided by the Bey of Tunisia to take the throne of Corsica, where he reigned for nine months in 1736.

33 **Bonneval** Claude Alexandre, Comte de Bonneval (1675–1747) was a French military officer who converted to Islam and served the Ottoman Empire. He appears in Casanova's autobiography.

33 **Cantacuzène** French spelling of the family name Cantacuzino. Perpessicius speculates that the reference is to Mihail Cantacuzino, ban of Craiova, who leaves Wallachia in 1776 and serves as a general to Catherine the Great.

33 **Tarakhanova** Isabella Tarakhanova (1755–1777) was the extramarital daughter of Empress Elizabeth Petrovna and Alexei Razumoski, a pretender to the Polish throne. She drowned when her St. Petersburg prison was flooded.

33 **the Duchess of Kingston** Elizabeth Chudleigh, Duchess of Kingston (1721–1788), was notorious for her amorous adventures; her trial for bigamy was watched by 4,000 people.

33 **the Chevalier d'Éon** Charles-Geneviève-Louis-Auguste-André-Timothée d'Éon de Beaumont (1728–1810) was a French diplomat and spy, who lived at different times as a man and as a woman.

33 **Zannowich** Stefano Zannowich (1751–1786), called "Hanibal," was a Serb writer and count from Montenegro. A gambler, counterfeiter, and socialite, he appears in Casanova's autobiography.

33 **Trenck** Friedrich von der Trenck (1726–1794) was a German mercenary and author who was arrested and beheaded in Paris during the French Revolution.

33 **Casanova** The Italian Giacomo Casanova (1725–1798) visited numerous European courts and was both a librarian and the author of an autobiography that includes portraits of many court adventurers and details of his love affairs.

33   **St. Germain**   The Count of St. Germain (1691–1784) claimed to be part of the noble Transylvanian Rákóczy family. A musician, spy, and visitor to European courts, he appears in Casanova's autobiography as a cosmetics peddler to royalty. He is later venerated by the theosophist Madame Blavatsky.

33   **Cagliostro**   Count Alessandro di Cagliostro (1743–1795) was an Italian magician and spiritualist to European courts; he also appears in Casanova's autobiography.

33   **Mesmer**   Franz Mesmer (1734–1815) was a Swabian doctor who studied what he called "animal magnetism." He treated groups of people through a *baquet*, a large tank with iron handles to conduct an energy he controlled.

33   **the bizarrities of Swedenborg**   Emanuel Swedenborg (1668–1772), a Swedish inventor and mystic, accurately predicted the date of his death.

33   **Schröpfer**   Johann Georg Schröpfer (1738–1774), German soldier, waiter, and spiritualist, died of a gunshot wound to the head.

33   **Scheele**   Carl Wilhelm Scheele (1742–1786) was a Swedish chemist who discovered oxygen prior to Lavoisier, with whom he was in communication. He was the author of *Chemical Treatise on Air and Fire* (1777), which upheld but diminished the existing phlogiston theory, postulating a substance released during combustion.

33   **Lavoisier**   Antoine Lavoisier (1743–1794) was a French chemist and biologist who recognized and named both oxygen and hydrogen; he opposed the phlogiston theory. He was arrested during the French Revolution and beheaded.

33   **Hoditz**   Albert Joseph von Hoditz (1706–1778) was an Austrian noble who lived off the income from his large and elaborate estate. He was an advocate of cremation.

33   **the falling King**   Gustav III (1746–1792), King of Sweden, was shot during a masked ball in Stockholm and died of the resulting infection.

33   **Anckarström**   Jacob Johan Anckarström (1762–1792), a Swedish military officer, was the confessed assassin of Gustav III; he was flogged and beheaded.

33   **the Lady of Lamballe**   Marie Thérèse Louise of Savoy (1749–1792), a close friend of Queen Marie Antoinette, was stabbed to death in the French Revolution; her decapitated head was paraded before Antoinette's prison window.

34   **Papura Jilava**   This is Mateiu's veiled reference to Ștefania Szekulics (1868–1926). Born in Bratislava to a German mother and Hungarian-Slovak father, and raised in Bucharest, she was a high-society theosophist and, under the name Bucura Dumbravă, a German-language novelist. Well connected politically, she founded the Chindia Society for the preservation of Romanian folk dances.

35   **"Ah, running after soldiers, the infantry, the cannoniers . . ."**   An army song of the time, popular after the 1877 war.

35   **Lamsdorf, Eulenburg, Metschersky were his spiritual fathers**   Vladimir Lamsdorf (1845–1907), Russian diplomat; Philipp Friedrich Alexander, Prince of Eulenburg and Hertefeld, Count of Sandels (1847–1912), German diplomat; Prince Vladimir Petrovich Meshchersky (1839–1914), Russian journalist. All were rumored or known to be gay.

35   **page-boys**   Mateiu uses a word from Ottoman, "icioglani," meaning "page" and carrying the association, as the context makes clear, of young men in politically advantageous sexual relationships with older men.

36   **"sketches"**   A genre favored by Mateiu's father, Ion Luca Caragiale.

37   **rachiu**   Pronounced "rahkyoo." A stronger version of țuica.

37   **opodeldoc**   Although the word refers to a variety of liniments, the term was created in the sixteenth century by Paracelsus as "oppodeltoch," to describe a combination of soap, camphor and alcohol, with wormwood as an option. As a friend writes me, "the word is an acronym from sweet myrrh, *Opo*panax chironium, b*del*lium, a myrrh-like gum, and Aris*toloch*ia."

38   **paparudas**   Women dressed only in branches, leaves, and vines, who dance through the village in times of drought to invoke the goddess of rain and fertility.

39   **raca**   An Aramaic insult that appears in Matthew 5:22, as part of the Sermon on the Mount: "But I say unto you, That whosoever is angry

with his brother without a cause shall be in danger of the judgment: and whosoever shall say to his brother, Raca, shall be in danger of the council: but whosoever shall say, Thou fool, shall be in danger of hell fire" (King James Version).

Confessions

41 **... sage citoyen du vaste univers.** "... wise citizen of the vast universe."

42 **"I am Greek"** In this chapter, Mateiu creates a contrast with other parts of the novel by including many Greek terms in Pantazi's account of his family. Some of these exist in English, though they are rare enough to require notes here. In my translation, I have also opted for words with Greek etymologies ("petrified," "catastrophe") where they were available.

42 **Even if I cannot be proud of my line** Here and elsewhere, Mateiu allows another character to take over the text from the narrator, omitting punctuation to mark a quotation.

44 **Prince Alexandru-Ioan** The Romanian politician and ruler Alexandru-Ioan Cuza (1820–1873) was elected prince of Moldavia and Wallachia in 1859 to unite the principalities, leading to the creation of Romania in 1862. He founded universities in Iaşi and Bucharest and was known for land reforms that led to his being deposed and exiled in 1866.

44 **yatak** A small sleeping area, sometimes a separate room, near the tiled stove that heats the house.

45 **cucoana** A term (from Greek) politely given to a married woman or a young woman from a noble family.

45 **the order of Nizan** An honorary order once awarded by the Bey of Tunisia.

47 **the yatagan** A sword associated with the Ottoman armies. Smaranda notes eight people executed by beheading. A "Mateist" might observe that of all the people Mateiu mentions in passing, which are noted here, eight were decapitated: Constantin Brâncoveanu, Inês de Castro, the Duke of Berwick, Friedrich von der Trenck, Antoine Lavoisier, Jacob Johan Anckarström, the Lady of Lamballe, and Saint Haralambie.

47 **Filiki Eteria** A secret anti-Ottoman society of diasporic Greeks, founded in 1814 in Odessa, active in Wallachia and Moldavia.

47 **Kaimakam** An Ottoman deputy.

48 **emancipation** The slavery of Roma people, and some people of the same social class called "*țigani*," was abolished in 1856. *Țigani* appear in property records in Wallachia as far back as the fourteenth century. According to nineteenth-century estimates, there were between 200,000 and 250,000 Roma in Romania, constituting about 6 percent of the population.

48 **a galben** A generic term for a gold-colored coin.

48 **The great Alexander Nikolayevich** Mateiu misspells this reference to Prince Alexander Mikhailovich Gorchakov (1798–1883), Russian statesman.

53 **ibrik** A small pot used for brewing coffee, whose shape, wider at its base than at its neck, allows the grounds to collect at the bottom as the coffee is poured off. The unfiltered coffee leaves dregs in the cup that can be used for divination, but the dregs in the pot are a mess to clean.

57 **refuge to a royal love** A reference again to Inês de Castro and Prince Pedro, who met at the estate called Quinta das Lagrimas.

59 **"Take's been wiped out."** The Romanian politician Take Ionescu (1858–1922) founded a new party in 1908, after a dispute over leadership of the Conservative Party. Mateiu's father was his supporter.

60 **Harpocrates** The Greek god of silence, represented as a curly-haired boy with his finger pointing to his chin (a precursor to holding a finger to the lips). Groucho Marx claims this god is the source of his silent brother's name. Harpo Marx disagrees.

61 **Profundum est cor super omnia—et homo est—et quis cognoscet eum?** "The heart is deep above all things—as is man—who can know it?" Mateiu's citation is more obscure than it seems. This Latin version of Jeremiah 17:9 does not follow the Vulgate, which reads, "Pravum est cor omnium, et inscrutabile: quis cognoscet illud?" or as the Douay-Rheims translates it, "The heart is perverse above all things, and unsearchable, who can know it?" Even though the reading "perverse" seems more aligned to Mateiu's taste, the variants "profundum" and "et homo est" show Mateiu is quoting a Latin ver-

sion of the Greek Septuagint. The first Romanian translation, the Bucharest Bible of 1688, was also made from the Septuagint, under the sponsorship of Şerban Cantacuzino and Constantin Brâncoveanu.

64 **grande mortalis aevi spatium**   From Tacitus's *Agricola*, book III: "A large part of a person's life."

66 **si Romae vivis, romano vivite more**   "When in Rome, do as the Romans do."

66 **Scipio Africanus**   Roman general (234–183 B.C.E.) who defeated Hannibal, was accused of graft, and died in exile.

Rakes' Twilight

69 **Vous pénétrerez dans les familles, nous peindrons des intérieurs domestiques, nous ferons du drame bourgeois de grandes et de petites bretêches.**   "You will be invited into the families' homes, we will paint the domestic scenes, we will make bourgeois dramas out of their fortifications both large and small." Charles Monselet (1825–1888) was a French novelist, poet, and playwright, known as "Le roi des gastronomes" for his food journalism.

69 **pulled the cross out first at the feast of the Baptism**   A tradition to celebrate the baptism of Jesus on January 6, in which a priest blesses a body of water by throwing in a cross. Whoever pulls it back out again enjoys a year of good luck.

71 **Crucea-de-piatră**   The Stone Cross is a famed interbellic red-light district in Bucharest.

72 **"Give, give my gun to me . . ."**   An anonymous Romanian poem from 1848, the year of the Wallachian Revolution.

72 **"You wit flowahs in your cap, you wit flowahs in your cap . . ."**   Pirgu (in a comical voice) sings a folk song about the life of a bandit. Ciotloş uncovered the text, which includes these lines: "My father and mother always ask me / what kind of work I like best! / The bandit's work, with a good horse / and flowers in your cap!"

75 **"piccolo, ma simpatico"**   Small, but nice.

76 **May 10th**   A former national holiday, Romanian Monarchy Day.

79 **the as yet un-united principalities** The principalities of Moldavia and Wallachia were united in 1859.

79 **logothete** Medieval title for chief minister.

83 **great-ban** Medieval title for a leader lower than the voivode.

84 **Monbijou** A palace in Berlin.

86 **"Vous devenez agaçant avec vos Arnoteano . . . Voyons, il faut être sérieux . . . Regardez, mon cher, quelle jolie femme, comme elle est jolie, elle est jolie comme tout! . . . Mais, mon pauvre ami, ne soyez pas idiot; vous êtes bête comme vos pieds! . . . Mais voyons, voyons.”** "You and your Arnoteanus are bothering me . . . Come on, let's be serious . . . Look, my dear, what a beautiful woman, how beautiful she is, more beautiful than anyone! . . . But my poor friend, don't be an idiot; you're as dumb as your shoes! . . . But calm down, calm down.”

87 **Saint Haralambie** An Orthodox saint, known as "Charalambos” in Greek, who was martyred by beheading in 201. In the Romanian tradition, he is a protector against disease.

88 **Bergson** French philosopher Henri Bergson (1859–1941).

88 **Hague Convention** The Hague Conventions of 1899 and 1907 established Europe's first international agreements on the laws of war.

88 **Piatra-Neamț** While this is an actual place in the north of Romania, its name, literally "the German Stone,” suggests here the stability and rationality stereotypically associated with Germans, the opposite of Bucharest's "Crucea-de-piatra.”

89 **Moldavian sun** Moldavia refers to the historical region and principality lying between the eastern Carpathian Mountains and the Dniester River; it joined with Wallachia in 1859 to form the United Principalities, which created their constitution in 1866, and whose capital in 1910 is Bucharest. Transylvania was added after World War I, forming the basis of modern Romania, eleven years before *Craii*'s publication and only two years before Mateiu begins the book's composition.

89 **belferiță** Ilinca uses a Romanianized version of the German word "*Beihelfer*.”

95 **Fomalhaut**   A bright autumn star, the first recorded star (beyond the sun) with an orbiting planet.

96 **phaeton**   A type of carriage.